THE WAITING GUN

OTHER FIVE STAR WESTERNS BY WAYNE D. OVERHOLSER:

THE WAITING GUN

A WESTERN STORY

WAYNE D. OVERHOLSER

FIVE STAR
A part of Gale, Cengage Learning

GALE
CENGAGE Learning®

Detroit • New York • San Francisco • New Haven, Conn • Waterville, Maine • London

GALE
CENGAGE Learning·

LIBRARY OF CONGRESS CATALOGING-IN-PUBLICATION DATA

Overholser, Wayne D., 1906–1996.
   The waiting gun : a western story / by Wayne D. Overholser.
   — 1st ed.
      p. cm.
   ISBN 978-1-4328-2625-3 (hardcover) — ISBN 1-4328-2625-5 (hardcover)
   1. Western stories. I. Title.
P53529.V33W26 2013
813'.54—dc23   2012032619

Published in conjunction with Golden West Literary Agency.
Find us on Facebook– https://www.facebook.com/FiveStarCengage
Visit our website– http://www.gale.cengage.com/fivestar/
Contact Five Star/ Publishing at FiveStar@cengage.com

Printed in Mexico
2 3 4 5 6 7 17 16 15 14 13

ADDITIONAL COPYRIGHT INFORMATION

CHAPTER ONE

Bill Varney and Shaniko Red had fine-combed Nevada Mesa from one end to the other for late calves that had been dropped after the regular spring roundup. They'd found a few, but not enough, and Bill knew that his dad, Old Mike Varney who owned Pitchfork, would howl his head off when he heard the number.

Old Mike had quite a few things to howl about these days. A slim calf crop, the low price of beef, a dry year and poor graze, the constant sniping from the small outfits south of Skull River—all added fuel to a temper that needed very little fuel to make it burst into a high flame.

Bill thought about this as he rode into camp with Shaniko Red the afternoon they wound up the job on the mesa. Old Mike would give him a cussing, letting on Bill was to blame for all that had gone wrong. That was Old Mike for you. He had to have a whipping boy, but it was never Bill's twin sister Vida, or Vida's husband-to-be, Turk Allen, who ramrodded the outfit. No, it was always Bill, and he'd had enough of it.

Not that it hit him suddenly. He'd never got along with Old Mike from the time he'd been a little shaver, partly because Vida had been the old man's favorite. Bill wasn't sure what the rest of it was due to unless his dad was jealous, afraid to have his boy grow up into a chip off the old block and challenge him. After Bill's mother had died a year ago, the situation had gone from bad to worse.

Bill reined up in front of the line cabin, motioning at Shaniko Red to stay on his horse. He said: "I'm hungry and tired and dirty, and I feel like cutting my wolf loose."

Shaniko was twenty-five, two years older than Bill, and his best friend. He was a good cowhand. No beauty, with a strawberry blotch on his left cheek and a mournful expression on his face that must have been there at birth, but he had all the sand in his craw a man could use, and just about the right proportion of caution, a quality Bill lacked.

"That's a proper feeling," Shaniko conceded, "seeing as we've been riding our tails off for about two weeks. I reckon we've got time to get to the ranch and tell Old Mike what we've done, and hike on into Broken Nose, but what in hell good could we do in that old maids' town?"

"I don't have any notion about riding into Broken Nose," Bill said. "I figured we'd have a swim in the river, and then pay the Hell Hole a visit."

Shaniko scratched his nose and scowled. The Hell Hole was a combination eating place, saloon, and gambling spot three miles down the river from Broken Nose. It was strictly off limits for anyone connected with Pitchfork, and Bill knew it as well as Shaniko did.

"I wouldn't mind that swim," Shaniko said, "but going on up to the Hell Hole is something else. You trying to get us fired?"

"Nope," Bill said. "I'm aiming to quit anyhow. I've had a bellyful."

He didn't feel like arguing about it, so he turned his buckskin and headed for the edge of the mesa. Shaniko could do what he damned well pleased. He was a hired hand and jobs were hard to come by. There was some sense in his hanging on, but it was different with Bill. He was a hired hand, too, and that was what put the burr under his blanket. He ought to be ramrodding the outfit, but no, it had to be Turk Allen who was just about as ornery a shorthorn as you could find in five counties.

Bill reached the rim and started down the mesa hill before Shaniko caught up with him. Bill had been pretty sure he'd come. If it toughed up to a showdown and Bill rode out, Shaniko would draw his time and ride along. That was the kind of hairpin he was. He wouldn't like it, but he'd do it.

They reached the county road and crossed it, pulling up under some cottonwoods. The day had been dry and hot just as every other day had been for over a month, but it was cool down here under the ancient trees, cool enough to feel like paradise after two weeks of hard riding up there on Nevada Mesa where there wasn't enough shade to cover a fair-size lizard.

Bill stepped down and began tugging off his boots. "Last man in has got a dirty neck," he said.

Shaniko didn't say a word and he didn't hurry. Bill beat him into the water by a good two minutes. They swam across the river and back, and crawled out to lie in the sand. The sun was almost down behind the high rims to the west.

"Let's get down to bedrock," Shaniko said. "You've been simmering for months. Now I ain't standing up for Old Mike. He's handed you the dirty end of the stick time after time, but you ain't got fifty dollars to your name. Where do you figure to go?"

"I don't know and I don't care," Bill said. "All I know is I've had enough of the old man's guff."

"We won't find nothing but trouble at the Hell Hole," Shaniko said. "Charlie Gilbert don't want no Pitchfork boys around. We'll wind up in a fight with Lud and there'll be hell to pay."

"You scared?"

"No, but. . . ."

"All right, then," Bill said. "Me, I figure a fight with Lud is just what the doctor ordered."

9

"Something else," Shaniko said. "What'll happen to your sis if you pull out?"

"You've always been sweet on her. You could stay and cut Turk out."

"A big chance I'd have," Shaniko said bitterly. "He's got her roped and tied, looks like."

"Well, I've said all I can to stop her. She's a big girl now."

Shaniko picked up a rock and threw it into the water. "There's another thing. Old Mike ain't gonna live forever. You pull out now and you'll be throwing your half of the outfit right down a gopher hole. You call that smart?"

"I don't give a damn how smart it is. I tell you I've had a bellyful."

Bill got up and began to dress.

Shaniko said: "I ain't blaming you, but I sure don't like to see you do something you'll be sorry for an hour after you ride off. You will be and don't you forget it."

"Why?"

"Because Old Mike's your dad."

"Wasn't his fault and it wasn't mine," Bill said testily. "Now quit preaching, will you? I'm gonna have myself a time tonight."

Shaniko let it go at that, but he rode along. Bill had a stubborn streak in him a foot wide, and, when he got the bit in his teeth and started to run, there wasn't much Shaniko or anyone else could do—anyone except Marian Tracey who ran a dressmaking shop in Broken Nose.

Bill had been in love with Marian for a long time, but he'd never quite got around to proposing. If he stayed on Pitchfork, he would. Shaniko was sure of that, providing she didn't get tired of waiting and marry the storekeeper, Phil Nider, who had been courting her for months.

So far Marian had shown no inclination to take Nider, so Shaniko figured Bill was her choice, if she had a chance to choose. More than once she'd slowed him down when he'd gotten some impractical scheme in his head. Shaniko considered riding into town and telling her how Bill was talking, then gave up the idea. He knew what Bill would say if he found out.

They crossed Sundog Creek that had dug the cañon between Nevada Mesa and Sundown Mesa on the east, and emptied into Skull River half a mile below the Hell Hole. The sun was showing a thin rind above the horizon when Bill and Shaniko reined up in front of the Hell Hole and tied. It was a ranch house on the river side of the road, dilapidated, and in need of paint, with some corrals and out buildings behind it.

It was ordinary enough in every way except for the tightly fenced pasture behind the house. The pasture held over a hundred calves, and the talk was that when a man wanted some fun in the Hell Hole, he found an unbranded Pitchfork calf, brought it in, and gave it to Charlie Gilbert, who slapped his brand on it and turned it into his pasture.

"Looks like we got the place to ourselves," Bill said. "Won't be no crowd, middle of the week this way."

"Good thing for us," Shaniko grumbled. "On a Saturday night they tell me there'll be twenty men here, all of 'em talking about how to bust Pitchfork and run the Varneys over the hill."

"Then it's time the Varneys came to them," Bill said.

The front door was open. Bill hadn't been in the house since Charlie Gilbert had bought it. Outside it appeared as rundown as ever, with half a dozen Plymouth Rock chickens scratching in the dust of the barren yard, and a scarred tomcat that sat on a corner of the porch giving himself a much needed bath.

The step to the porch trembled under Bill's weight. "Somebody's going to break his leg on this thing," he said.

"Be lucky if we don't get more'n a leg busted before we get out of here," Shaniko said gloomily.

The interior of the house had been worked over. The partition between what had been a parlor and the front bedroom had been torn out so now it was one big room that took up the entire front of the house, a bar on one side, a couple of tables near the kitchen door, and several green-topped poker tables on the other side of the room.

Neither Charlie Gilbert nor his boy Lud was in sight, but Annie Bain was. She worked behind the bar when needed, or cooked and served a meal, or, as Gilbert bragged, humored any desire a man might have. All part of the Hell Hole's service, Gilbert claimed. A man could find anything here he wanted, from a poker game with the sky the limit on down to a thick steak fried the way mother used to.

Annie got up from the table where she'd been sitting, reading a month-old Denver newspaper. "What'll it be, boys?" she asked genially. "You name it. We got it."

She was a big woman, thirty or more, but well put together, and attractive, if a man liked his women loud and flamboyant. She had too much powder on her face and too much rouge on her cheeks to suit Bill, but he guessed he was a little finicky when it came to women.

"Steak," Bill said. "Rare enough to fight back at you."

"The same," Shaniko said.

"Just the way I like it." Annie stepped to the bar. "Have a drink first, boys?"

"Why sure," Bill said. "Now about that steak. Been so long since we've had a good meal that. . . ."

"Don't you worry yourself none." Annie poured their drinks and set the bottle on the rough pine bar. "I'll go get your steaks started."

"Pitchfork beef?" Bill asked.

"Sure it's Pitchfork beef," Annie said flippantly. "Reckon you're strangers. Nobody on Skull River eats anything but Pitchfork beef."

She went into the kitchen, walking with surprising grace for a big woman. Bill picked up his glass and nodded at Shaniko. "Mud in your eye," he said, and drank.

"Reckon Annie don't know us," Shaniko said.

"Didn't act like it." Bill laughed. "Wouldn't Old Mike raise Cain if he heard what Annie said?"

"Aw, she was just joshing." Shaniko picked up the bottle and glass and, carrying them to a table, sat down. Bill followed, shaking his head. He said: "Shaniko, that worried look you've got on your face would sour the cream in a Jersey before it ever got into the bucket."

"Reckon it would," Shaniko agreed, "but I didn't like this notion when you first got it, and nothing's happened since to make me like it. Purty soon Charlie's gonna walk in here and he'll blow the roof off when he sees who Annie's feeding."

"Let him blow." Bill leaned back and rolled a smoke. "I've been thinking about him. Maybe he's got cause to rustle our calves . . . *if* he is doing it."

He poured himself a drink, then sat back, his eyes on the amber-colored liquid. Old Mike had handled Charlie Gilbert the same way he handled everyone and everything he didn't like. Gilbert had drifted into Broken Nose more than a year ago with Annie Bain and his boy Lud, and applied for a license to start a saloon.

As far back as Bill could remember, there had been just the one saloon in Broken Nose, the Stockade, owned and operated by Chauncey Morts who was a friend of Old Mike's. Morts didn't cotton to competition, so Old Mike saw to it that the town council boosted the license fee to $1,000. Gilbert couldn't pay the freight, but instead of leaving, he simply moved down river and started the Hell Hole.

Annie came in and lit the wall lamps. "Your supper's almost ready," she said in her cheerful tone, and returned to the kitchen.

Bill pushed his long legs under the table and relaxed. Watching him, Shaniko marveled that he had stayed on Pitchfork as long as he had. He stood a good six feet, and in spite of the deceiving appearance of his thin, almost gaunt, face, he weighed one hundred seventy-five pounds, much of it in his hard-muscled shoulders.

His hair was on the sandy side, he had more freckles than the law allowed any one man, and his eyes, dark blue, now seemed almost black in the lamplight. He downed his drink, set the glass back, and began tapping the table with his fingertips. He was not a nervous man, but he was nervous now, and Shaniko recognized it as a sign of the pressure that was building up in him.

Annie came in with her arms full of dishes and set them in front of both men. She returned with their coffee and pie. Bill covered his steak with ketchup and began to eat, nodding at Annie who hovered over them.

"So this is how you built your reputation," Bill said when his mouth was empty.

"That's it, mister," Annie said with pride. "Nothing too good for our customers."

She sat down at the other table and watched them eat, making small talk and demanding nothing in reply. She was a pleasant woman who apparently expected little from life and was satisfied with what she had. The vitriolic bitterness that had goaded Charlie Gilbert into staying on Skull River and running the Hell Hole did not seem to be in his woman.

"You boys looking for a job?" Annie asked finally.

"No, not here," Bill said.

"Drifting through, I reckon," she said. "Headed for Utah, maybe."

"Maybe," Bill said, and finished his pie. He dropped a couple of silver dollars on the table, a little disappointed that Charlie

Gilbert hadn't shown up. "That enough?"

"Plenty," she said. "Sure you boys don't want nothing else?"

"Nothing else," Shaniko said. "We'll be going along."

Bill got up, then stood motionless, his gaze on the kitchen doorway. Charlie Gilbert stood there, his big body filling it, tiny black eyes squinting at Bill. "Well, Annie," he said, "you know whose gut you've been filling?"

"Just a couple of drifters," she said.

"No, you're a little wrong," Gilbert said. "This here is Old Mike's pup and his friend, Shaniko Red, right off Pitchfork range." He turned his head and called: "Lud, come here!"

CHAPTER TWO

A great laugh broke out of Bill Varney, a joyful laugh that came from far down in his throat. "Yeah, Lud, you come on out," he said.

He didn't notice Annie Bain slip behind him to the bar and pick up a shotgun. She pointed it at Shaniko Red as she pronged back the hammer, motioning for him to stand where he was.

Bill kept his eyes on Charlie Gilbert in the doorway and Lud who stood behind him. Bill didn't think this was headed toward gun play. Neither Charlie nor Lud were noted for their fast draws, but they were barroom brawlers of the first order. If they both jumped him, he was in for trouble.

Charlie moved toward Annie who stood at the end of the bar. He was a big man who would probably weigh two hundred fifty pounds or better, much of it fat from the easy living around the roadhouse. He had an overly large head that was as round and hairless as a child's rubber ball. His faded blue eyes, partly hidden behind rolls of fat, gave the lie to the old saying that fat men were pleasant and easy going. His eyes were filled with an animosity that was animal-like in its ferocity.

"You've got a lot of gall coming here, Varney," Gilbert said. "Trying to spy on us for your old man?"

"Nothing like that, Charlie," Bill said. "Shaniko 'n' me just got hungry for somebody else's cooking and we heard Annie put out good meals."

Gilbert placed his right hand against the bar, palm down,

16

plainly a little uncertain. Lud edged forward, a small grin on his bulldog face. He was a younger edition of his father, hair on his head and without the fat, but driven by the same ruthless brutality that was in his father.

"I sure don't savvy," Charlie said. "You know you ain't welcome, and I heard your old man gave orders that any Pitchfork man who came here got fired."

"That's right," Bill said, "but we didn't figure you'd tell anybody we'd been here." He glanced at Lud, and then back to Charlie. "Maybe you don't figure on telling. Maybe Lud's just going to beat me up. That it?"

"Charlie, tell Annie to get this shotgun off me," Shaniko said, "and we'll mosey on. We had our meal and we paid. You've got no cause to make a fight of it."

"You think not, after what Old Mike done to me?" Charlie demanded, his uncertainty leaving him. "Well, sir, that old bastard ain't got much more'n twelve hours to live. Don't see no reason why his kid should live that long. Git him, Lud."

Lud's grin widened as he lumbered forward, huge fists cocked in front of him. Bill laughed in his face as he ducked an uppercut that Lud started from his knees and threw his own right that squashed Lud's nose like an overripe plum.

"Come on, Lud," Bill taunted. "Come and git me like your pappy said."

Lud blinked in surprise and wiped his bloody nose, driven back on his heels by that flicking right that was like a darting shadow but packed the wallop of a mule kick. He swung again and missed. Bill charged in and nailed him with a right and a left that rocked his head, then leaped back out of the other man's reach.

"Git in there, Lud!" Charlie yelled. "What the hell's the matter with you? Need some help?"

"No," Lud said thickly between rapidly swelling lips. "I'll take him."

He rushed again, trying to get his hands on Bill, but Bill spun away, timing his move perfectly, and Lud, carried forward by the momentum of his charge, hit the wall with a resounding crash and was knocked flat on his back.

"Let's drift, Shaniko," Bill said. "This isn't a fight. I don't want to hurt him."

"Not till Annie gets her damned scatter-gun off my brisket," Shaniko said. "She acts like she wants me for breakfast."

Lud lay on the floor where he had fallen, blood a scarlet mask on his face. Charlie grabbed an empty whiskey bottle off a shelf behind the bar. "You ain't going nowhere, bucko," he said, and started for Bill with the bottle raised over his right shoulder.

Bill slipped around him toward the kitchen door, realizing for the first time this was more than a fight. Charlie Gilbert aimed to kill him, and he might do it when Lud got to his feet if Shaniko was kept out of it.

"You made a mistake getting that bottle, Charlie," Bill said, backing toward the table where he'd eaten his supper. "If you aim to get ornery, I will, too."

Charlie said nothing. He swung around and moved toward Bill with ponderous, dogged persistence. Bill backed up until he hit the table. He grabbed a chair with his right hand, twisting sideways as Charlie swung the bottle. Charlie missed, stumbled into the table, and sent dishes clattering. He fell forward, half his body draped across the table, just as Bill swung the chair, smashing him in the small of his back.

Shaniko yelled a warning, but it got through to Bill too late. Lud had been stunned briefly. Now he was on his feet and this time he got his hands on Bill, big arms around his waist with his fists pressing into Bill's stomach, and tried to wrestle him to the floor.

"Get out of it, Bill!" Shaniko yelled. "He'll kill you like that! Bust out of it!"

But there was no breaking out of the bear-like hug. Lud had an advantage in weight and strength, and, when he failed to get Bill off his feet, he seemed content to squeeze, knowing that it was all he needed to do.

Bill twisted and squirmed, plunging wildly in a frantic effort to break loose, but the great arms held like a vise, the pressure steadily increasing. Bill slammed his head back, striking Lud's battered, bloody nose; he stomped a boot heel down on the arch of Lud's foot. The blow must have sent pain racketing up the man's leg, but he didn't slacken his grip.

There was no breath in Bill's lungs now, no strength in his body to fight. He was like a drowning man going down for the third time. He went slack in Lud's arms. Lud released his grip, took Bill by the shoulder as he started to fall, and, whirling him around, hit him fully in the face.

Annie cried out. For the moment her eyes were on Lud and Bill, not Shaniko, who had been slowly edging toward her. She called: "Lud, that's enough!" Shaniko took the long step to the bar and batted the shotgun aside with one hand.

Instinctively Annie pulled the trigger; the buckshot ripped into the floor. Shaniko twisted the gun out of her hands just as Lud wheeled to face him. Shaniko let him have it on the side of the head with the barrel, sending him reeling back toward the poker tables on the far side of the room.

Shaniko threw the shotgun at him and yanked his Colt from leather as Annie came charging out from behind the bar. Shaniko faced her, the six-gun in his hand.

"I've never killed a woman, but, by God, I'll start now if you don't behave!" Shaniko motioned for her to step back. "They aimed to kill Bill and they'd have killed me. I figured Old Mike was wrong about these two bastards, but I missed it. We're gonna have to run 'em clean out of the country."

Charlie pulled himself upright and leaned against the wall, groaning with every move. Apparently he couldn't straighten up. He whimpered: "The son-of-a-bitch broke my back with that chair. I'll get him, Shaniko. I'll cut his heart out. That's a promise."

Annie retreated to her place behind the bar. Lud sat down at one of the poker tables and began to dab at his face with a red bandanna that was being turned a brighter red by the blood pouring from his nose and a long cut on the side of one cheek.

"Ain't much fight left in this outfit, Bill," Shaniko said. "They asked for trouble and they sure got a dose of it. I reckon it's time for us to go."

Bill got to his feet and staggered toward the front door. He stumbled and fell flat on his face, got up again and, reaching the door, gripped the casing and held himself upright. Shaniko retreated toward him, gaze moving from Annie to Charlie to Lud and back to Charlie.

"Makes me no never mind whether I kill one of you or not," Shaniko said. "Fact is, I would if I had my druthers, but it might kick up some dust with the sheriff, so I won't, if you don't make me." Reaching the door, he put his left hand on Bill's shoulder. "You all right?"

"I think so," Bill muttered. "Can't get my breath good. Must have some broken ribs."

"We're about to shake the dust of this stinking place off our feet," Shaniko said. "Get on your horse. Charlie, I'll tell you what I'm going to do. I'm going out there and get on my horse. You'd better hug the floor 'cause I'm going to let go with a few slugs. Through the door and through the windows. If you're more'n two feet high, you'll sure as hell spring a leak."

Bill was breathing easier now. He crossed the yard to his horse, the yard rising and falling before him so that everything

20

in front of him—horses and cottonwoods and the hitch pole—all seemed distorted and out of focus. He untied his horse and got into the saddle just as Shaniko ran out of the house.

"Move!" Shaniko yelled. "Damn it, bust a hole in the breeze!"

Bill put his horse into a gallop, going downstream. He almost fell out of the saddle. He gripped the horn and rode bent forward, his ribs hurting him with every jump of his horse. Shaniko was in the saddle then. He let go with five shots, one through the door waist high, two through each window. A moment later he caught up with Bill, saying: "Slow down. They ain't hungering for trouble enough to come after us. Didn't look to me like there was enough fight left in that bunch to take on an undersize fly."

Bill reined his horse down to a walk. They splashed across Sundog Creek, and went on until they reached the foot of the trail that came down the mesa hill from the line cabin. Bill pulled up. "I've got to get down for a while," he said. "Every time my horse takes a step, I feel like I've got ten thousand knives sticking into me."

He carefully dismounted, leaving the reins dragging, and, kneeling at the edge of the river, scooped water over his face. Shaniko said: "You figured a fight with Lud would be just what the doctor ordered, but looks to me like you'd better order the doctor."

"Sure, sure," Bill said irritably. "Rub it in. How'd I know they'd gang up on me?"

"You should've known," Shaniko snapped. "We just about got our goose cooked. We would have, if Sid Kehoe or some of the rest of them greasy-sack ranchers on the other side of the river had been there." A moment of silence, Bill not saying anything, then Shaniko asked: "Still gonna ride out in the morning?"

"Sure, soon as I get my time."

"What do you figure Charlie meant by saying Old Mike don't have much more'n twelve hours to live?"

"Dunno. Just talking, maybe."

"More'n that," Shaniko said stubbornly. "There's just two ways of looking at Old Mike. You bow down to him like he wants you to, maybe because he's paying your wages or you know your bread's buttered on the Pitchfork side, or you hate him like hell. If you hate him long enough like Charlie Gilbert has, you're gonna do something about it. I figure Charlie's finally got there."

"Nothing he can do," Bill said.

Bill got up and, getting back into the saddle, started up the trail, Shaniko behind him.

"Never knew you to ride out on a fight," Shaniko said. "And we got one coming. Otherwise them Gilberts wouldn't have jumped us. Take the little fry. Box H. The Lazy L. Kehoe's Wineglass spread. Old Mike's been accusing 'em of rustling Pitchfork beef, Kehoe especially. He's gobbled up everything on this side of the river, so they know that sooner or later he's gonna move over to their side. Only adds up one way, Bill."

Still Bill said nothing as his horse labored up the twisting trail. He wished Shaniko would shut his mouth. He didn't owe Old Mike a damned thing. His dad had made that mighty clear. He had a job on Pitchfork. No more and no less. He had absolutely no understanding of the voracious appetite for land that seemed to be a consuming fire in the old man.

Bill's mother had never understood it, either. Many times she'd said: "Mike's like a rig running downhill, going faster and faster, and now he can't stop." Then she'd add: "Don't ever get that way, Bill. It's no way to live."

She'd been right. As Bill thought about her, it seemed to him she'd been right about everything. By some miracle she'd been able to retain her serenity and peace of mind, making do with what she had and being happy with it.

Bill didn't know for sure, but he thought that something must have happened back in their early years on Skull River, something that had pulled them in opposite directions—Old Mike to wealth and power, Bill's mother to her housework and chickens and garden. For years they hadn't slept in the same bed; they hadn't even talked to each other unless it had been absolutely necessary.

Another thing that had always puzzled Bill was the fact that he had been able to talk to his mother and she to him, but he'd found no common ground with Old Mike. The odd part of it was that his twin sister Vida had hated housework and chickens and garden, and, as she grew older, she seemed to have more in common with Old Mike and less with her mother.

He topped the rim and pulled up on the level ground. Someone was in the line cabin. The lamp was burning, the door open so a yellow patch of light stained the ground in front of the cabin. A moment later Shaniko reached him and stopped, too.

"Who do you reckon is calling on us?" Bill asked.

"Dunno, but it ain't trouble or there wouldn't be a light."

Bill considered that a moment. Shaniko might be right, but then again, whoever it was might be hoping to pull them into the light and start shooting. That was the trouble with being named Varney. You inherited all the enemies Old Mike had. For the moment Bill felt he'd had all the trouble he wanted.

"Hello!" Bill called. "Who's there?"

His sister Vida appeared in the doorway. "About time you got back," she said. "Where have you been?"

Bill rode on to the cabin, so relieved that he was physically weak. "Didn't figure on you calling this time of night," Bill said as he swung down. "We finished today, so we went down and had a swim and supper in the Hell Hole."

"Wound up in a tussle," Shaniko added. "Bill had to work the bile out of his system, which he done."

"The Hell Hole," Vida said in disgust. "If you aren't a pair of fools. You know what Dad will say?"

"I'll take care of your horse," Shaniko said to Bill as if glad to escape a family quarrel.

He rode toward the corral, leading Bill's buckskin. Bill went past Vida into the cabin and sprawled on his bunk. "I don't rightly care what the old man says. I'm quitting. I figure Shaniko will go with me."

Vida stood in the middle of the room, staring at him, her hands on her hips. She was a tall girl, with strong features dominated by a wide chin. She was perfectly proportioned, an attractive woman even as she was now—wearing a divided tan skirt, a calfskin vest, and work-scarred boots. In many ways she was willful because Old Mike had spoiled her, but still she was honest and decent and she loved Bill even if he thought Turk Allen was low enough to crawl under a snake's belly without touching the peak of his Stetson.

But this was too much and she began to swell with righteous anger. Bill said wearily: "I don't want to hear it, Vida. I damned near got killed tonight." He sat up and took off his shirt. "Fetch that bottle of liniment yonder on the shelf and give me a rub. If I don't have some cracked ribs, I'll be all right, come morning."

"You'd better be," she said angrily. "I never heard such stupid talk in my life. You can't just ride off like . . . like one of the crew."

She began to rub his back with strong, skillful hands. It seemed to Bill that he felt better at once, that each motion of her hands brought strength to him. Then she stepped back, corking the bottle of liniment and putting it on the table.

"They're fixing to kill Dad in the morning and he's stubborn enough to let them do it," she said. "You know how he's been crippled up with rheumatism the last year or so. You've got to save his life."

CHAPTER THREE

Bill slept very little that night. He was kept awake not by his sore muscles as much as by the question that had plagued him for a long time. How much did a son owe his father, particularly when the father seemed to feel he owed nothing to his son?

He couldn't forget what Shaniko Red had said earlier in the evening, that he'd be sorry he'd ridden off before he was gone an hour. And why? Simply because Old Mike was his father. Nothing could change the accident of birth, an accident that forced a certain amount of loyalty upon a man whether the family relationship warranted that loyalty or not.

According to Vida's story, a gunslinger named Ace Kehoe was in Broken Nose. He had come to town for the express purpose of shooting Old Mike. He had sent Old Mike a letter calling him every name in the book, and he had spread the word around Broken Nose that the old man was too yellow to meet him.

The only surprising thing about this was that it hadn't happened a long time ago, with Old Mike running roughshod over everybody within a hundred miles the way he had. Ace Kehoe's brother Sid, who owned Wineglass, was one of the greasy-sack ranchers who lived across the river south of town. Old Mike had branded him a rustler and ordered him out of the country. When he hadn't gone, the bank had cut off his credit. When he still didn't go, Turk Allen caught him in town one day and gave him a beating that put him in bed.

It struck Bill that, if he were Sid Kehoe, he'd have sent for his brother, too. If he were any of the small ranchers south of the river, or if he were Charlie Gilbert, he'd feel the same way they did. But this feeling didn't change anything; it did not excuse outright murder. And it would be murder, with Old Mike slowed by rheumatism and going against a man like Ace Kehoe who made a living from his gun.

Bill stared into the darkness while the slow hours ran their course. He could hear Vida's steady breathing from the other bunk. Shaniko Red was sleeping outside somewhere. He'd had no part in the argument. He'd had his say earlier in the evening. He wouldn't go over it again.

There were other men on Pitchfork who could face Ace Kehoe, and with a little luck come out alive. Shaniko was one. Dutch John was another. So was Turk Allen. Any of them would do it, if Vida asked them, but she wouldn't because she felt it was Bill's responsibility.

"I don't want you killed," she'd said. "If I thought you would be, I wouldn't have come here asking you to fight Kehoe. If I were a man, I'd do it. It boils down to just one thing, Bill. You're Dad's only son."

Well, he couldn't argue with that. He had the best chance, too, although Vida hadn't said it. He knew he was faster with a gun than anyone else on Pitchfork. So he was the natural choice, either way you looked at it.

Yet there was a nasty doubt in his mind that persisted in spite of his efforts to ignore it—that if he were killed, all of Pitchfork would go to Vida. Old Mike was sixty-five. He wouldn't live many more years. And maybe, aside from that, Vida would rather have Bill risk his life than Turk Allen, the man she was going to marry. Still worse was the fact that Old Mike wouldn't appreciate anyone, and that included his son, taking his fight off his hands, even when it meant saving his life.

So the thoughts revolved through Bill's mind like the slow turning of a wheel, always coming back to Vida's one short sentence: "You're Dad's only son."

He got up with the first dawn light and built a fire. The racket at the stove woke Vida. She sat up, asking: "Are you going to do it?"

"I'll do it," he said. "I reckon you knew I would."

She crossed the room to him and hugged him. "Yes, I knew you would. I've heard Dad say more than once that you had more sand in your craw than any other man he knows."

He turned away from her, convinced she was lying. Old Mike, as far as he knew, had never said a good word about him from the day he'd matched the old man's height, a splinter of a kid who had thought proudly at the time that he had the world by the tail and a downhill pull.

"I'll do it, and then I'm getting out," he said. "I told you that last night and nothing's changed."

"You can't, Bill." She caught his shoulder. "We're your family. We love you. I know Dad doesn't show it, but he does. I don't know why he acts the way he does. Sometimes I think you're too much alike."

"The hell we are!" he said savagely. "You think I'd tromp on everybody the way he does? If it was me, I'd have been satisfied with Pitchfork a long time ago." He poured water from the bucket into the coffee pot and set it on the front of the stove. He looked at her, thinking how much she was like Old Mike, but she didn't know it. The small regret he had about leaving was on account of her. They'd grown up together. She'd been a tomboy when she was a kid. They'd gone fishing together and hunting; they'd laughed and they'd played and they'd fought. They'd taken each other for granted, and suddenly it hit him, sharply and poignantly, that he'd miss her, more even than Marian Tracey. He'd never been quite sure he wanted Marian for a wife, but, if he decided he did, the decision to ask her would be his to make. On the other hand, he had Vida for his sister, an accident of birth just as Old Mike had been given to him for a father.

"Vida." He reached out with both hands and then dropped them, his old habit of not showing any affection overriding this sudden impulse. "You can't marry Turk Allen. He's no good. For you or any other woman. He's not even a good ramrod. Shaniko will tell you that. Any of the boys will."

She whirled and walked back to her bunk, sat down, and pulled on her boots. She said: "Let's not go over that again. I'm marrying Turk in September."

"He's been pushing up the date, hasn't he?"

"How did you know?"

"I figured it'd be like him. He doesn't want to take any chances on losing you or your share of Pitchfork. In time you'll find out what he is. After you're married it'll be too late."

"Oh, stop it, Bill," she said wearily. "I'll get breakfast. Go out and get Shaniko."

"Do you love Turk?"

"I won't even discuss it. Go get Shaniko."

"Do you love him? Damn it, answer me."

"Of course, I love him," she said defiantly. "Do you think I'd be engaged to him if I didn't? Do you think I'd set a date in September if I didn't?"

He walked to the door, knowing he had gained nothing by bullying her. Once she had taken her stand, she'd never be able to back down from it, even if she knew she was wrong.

He hesitated at the door, then turned back. "How do you figure on working it? Dad'll raise hell if he knows what I'm going to do."

"He won't know," she said. "We'll stop at Nider's store and go in. Nider's got a new mowing machine he wants Dad to see.

He sent word back with me the last time I was in town. You tell Dad you're going to see Marian."

Bill nodded and went outside. Again the doubts nagged him. She had it figured out right down to a gnat's eyebrow. Maybe she did want him killed. Then he was ashamed. Vida had never lied to him, or even tricked him. He didn't believe she was capable of it.

Shaniko Red was awake and washing at the spring back of the cabin. When he saw Bill, he asked: "You taking the job on?"

"Yeah, and don't tell me you knew all the time I would."

"Why, hell no," Shaniko said amiably. "I figured this was the day we were giving up our soft jobs and riding out to make our fortunes."

"Tomorrow'll do." Bill jerked his head at the cabin. "Come on."

They left after breakfast, the sun barely showing above the Flat Tops far up Skull River. They didn't take the regular roundabout trail that led off Nevada Mesa to the river, then along Skull past the Hell Hole and up the wagon road which led from the river to Pitchfork. Instead, they took the short way, directly east and down the steep slope to Sundog Creek and on up the other side to Sundown Mesa. There was no trail this way, and shale on both sides of the creek made the going slow and dangerous, but it was faster than the long way, and this morning time was an important factor. Besides, if they followed the county road that ran in front of the Hell Hole, they'd probably be shot out of their saddles by the Gilberts. It would be a finish fight the next time they met the Gilberts. Bill didn't have any doubt of that. He couldn't risk it this morning with Vida along.

So they took the short way and crossed the creek where it ran, clear and swift, a mile above the river. The bottom of the cañon still held the early morning shadows, and the light was so thin that Bill barely caught the dark streaks made by frightened trout as they darted across the shallows toward the deep pool upstream from the horses. Memories touched him, sharp and very clear, of fishing in Sundog Creek with Vida when they were kids, and of the beatings Old Mike had given him because he hadn't done the work he was supposed to. But not Vida. Anything she did was all right with Old Mike.

They climbed the east wall of the cañon, twisting back and forth. The muscles of their horses knotted as they labored up the steep slope. They stopped several times for their horses to blow, and Vida shook her head at Bill, her face showing the strain of uncertainty.

"They may get started ahead of us," Vida said. "I didn't tell Dad or Turk where I was going."

"We'll catch them," Bill said.

A few minutes later they topped the rim and struck off across the mesa. The Pitchfork buildings were directly in front of them. A sharp ridge rose just north of the buildings, the top dark with close-growing cedars. A spring broke out of the rocks up there near the top of the ridge and made a fair-size stream that flowed past the house.

That source of good water was the primary reason Old Mike had picked this spot for his headquarters more than twenty years ago. Cottonwoods that he had planted at the time had been hardly more than switches, but now they were sizable trees that laid a pleasant shade across the front yard.

Just as with the cottonwoods, everything Old Mike had done had been with an eye to the future. Even though he had been short of money at first, he had threatened, begged, borrowed, or stolen enough to start with a fair-size herd. He had put up buildings he'd need ten years in the future. The result was that he had not been forced to build since then. Old Mike had simply laid out his dream and then grown into it.

The stark efficiency of the ranch always struck Bill when he approached it, even as familiar with the outfit as he was. Nothing out of place, everything clean, but no foofaraw, either. Even the flowers that Bill's mother used to tend were not in evidence this summer. The long log house, bunkhouse, cook shack, sprawling barns, the solid corrals—all added up to the same thing, a ranch designed and operated for practical purposes and no sentiment.

Old Mike and Turk Allen were saddling up when Vida, Bill, and Shaniko Red rode into the yard. Old Mike faced them, his tough, dark face hardening, his down-slanting white mustache seeming to bristle with temper. This was the front he always showed the world, whether to a crowd or a single rider, or even Bill alone. It was not because of any nervousness that was in him. He simply could not change, even knowing he would die within the next two or three hours. Except with Vida. Bill had never seen him show the slightest tenderness or gentleness with anyone else.

Old Mike pinned his faded blue eyes on Bill. "What are you two doing here?"

"We got done," Bill said, "so, when Vida showed up last night, I figured I'd ride into town with you."

"This ain't a Saturday to blow in town." Old Mike jerked a thumb toward the ridge north of the house. "You 'n' Shaniko hightail back there. Dutch John and Birnie Hanks can use a little help."

Bill shook his head. "I'm going with you. I figure to see Marian."

"The hell you are!" Old Mike bellowed. "By God, you're still taking orders from me!"

Bill glanced at Turk Allen, who had finished tightening his cinch and had turned amused eyes on the old man. He knew when to talk and when to listen, and that was one of the reasons they got along. He was a blocky man, shorter than Bill but heavier. He wore a full black mustache and sideburns, an affectation that irritated Bill for no good reason. Allen's ruddy face always glowed with good humor, and that irritated Bill, too, because it was as false as the ring of a counterfeit dollar on a cherry-wood bar.

"This is an order I'm not taking," Bill said. "No use pushing."

Old Mike began to swell the way he did when he was crossed, his eyes catching fire so they momentarily lost their faded look. Bill thought: *This is my father whose life I'm going to save while I risk my own.* The bile of bitterness washed through him as he leaned forward, defiantly meeting his father's gaze, knowing he could not back down after promising Vida.

"He's been over there on Nevada Mesa for two weeks," Vida said. "That's a long time for him not to see his girl."

She had a way of touching the old man when no one else could. He shrugged as if it had suddenly become a minor matter. "All right, ride along, if it's that important," Old Mike said. "How many calves did you brand?"

"Eleven," Bill said.

The old man began to swell again. "Eleven!" he shouted. "By God, two hundred missing and you found eleven! What were you doing, sitting on your . . . ?"

"No, we worked," Shaniko said.

To his surprise, Bill sensed a note of resentment in the cowboy's voice. He never had before when Shaniko was forced to listen to Old Mike's outbursts.

"All right." Old Mike jerked his thumb in the direction of the ridge again. "You'll find Dutch John and Birnie on the other side of the stone cabin."

For a moment Shaniko Red's gaze met Bill's. He nodded as if to say: "Good luck."—and wheeled his horse and rode away.

Old Mike mounted, calling—"Let's ride!"—and turned his horse toward the wagon road that led to the river.

Turk Allen stepped up and rode beside the old man, and Vida and Bill came behind. Neither spoke for a time, then Vida said in a low tone: "I won't blame you if you leave tomorrow. He had no call to act the way he did."

This was the first time he had ever heard her censure Old Mike. She was probably the only living person who loved him, and, if he turned her against him, there would be no one. For twenty years he had worked at building a fortune, and he had worked equally hard at destroying himself. Now, staring at his wide back, at the domineering way he held his head, Bill felt sorry for him.

Old Mike reined up before they started down the long grade that was a shelf cut out of the side of the mesa hill. He stared at the Hell Hole directly below them, then he said to Turk Allen: "Who'll be home tonight?"

"Dutch John, Birnie Hanks, and Shaniko Red." Allen jerked his head at Bill. "And him."

"Soon as it's dark," Old Mike said, "you take 'em and clean out that place. Burn it to the ground." Then he started down the road that bent at this point, angling southeast down the hill until it struck the county road.

He had given the order, Bill thought, as casually as he would lay out the work orders for the day.

CHAPTER FOUR

Phil Nider woke with the delicious knowledge that this was the day Old Mike Varney was to die. He dressed slowly and carefully as he always did, then shaved before he went downstairs to the breakfast that his housekeeper, Mrs. O'Toole, always had ready exactly at 8:00 A.M.

For more than a year Nider had been able to take his time in the morning the way a successful merchant should. That was when Carl Akins had gone to work for him. Carl could be depended upon to open the store at 8:00, regardless of the weather, his health, or anything else. So Phil Nider, precise, neat, and blessed with a memory that never forgot a slight or a favor, was able to dawdle each morning, secure in the knowledge that business would go on as usual.

This morning Nider took a little more time before going down the stairs. He studied himself in the mirror, thinking with satisfaction that he appeared younger than forty-five, that folks in Broken Nose never thought of him as being that old. Take Marian Tracey. Just the other day she'd said he didn't look a day over thirty. She'd make a beautiful bride, he thought. All he needed was a little more patience, a little more assistance from her mother, and most of all a little more neglect on the part of young Bill Varney.

Before he went downstairs, he took his pearl-handled .44 out of a bureau drawer and ran the fingers of his left hand over the long barrel. He was a good shot and he was not a coward. For years he had fought the temptation to take this gun and jump Old Mike Varney and kill him just as Ace Kehoe was going to do today.

He had never quite been able to bring himself to do it, partly because of the way he had felt about Old Mike's wife, and partly because he didn't want to destroy the life he had built for himself here in Broken Nose.

What people saw was an illusion. They considered him a slender, not very strong man, a little on the dude side, but with high morals, a counter jumper who was too squeamish to chop off a rooster's head. They trusted him, even liked him because he was liberal with credit, and he was confident he was the last man in the country that anyone would suspect of having been a train robber in his youth.

Well, a man had to get his start some way, and Nider had never regretted using the method he had. He enjoyed the respect folks had for him, enjoyed living the relaxed and comfortable life of a man who had nothing to fear from the law, and he particularly enjoyed the satisfaction that came from fooling everybody.

One by one the men he had ridden with had met violent deaths, but he'd been smart enough to quit at the right time. So he had been loath to do anything that would change people's opinion of him.

In the long run it was better to put up with Old Mike Varney, to show him a polite front, while all the time to hate him with a passion that burned a little hotter on each occasion when he met the old pirate face to face and treated him with the deference he expected.

He replaced the gun, satisfied that today he would accomplish his purpose without having to pull the trigger himself. He put on his steel-rimmed spectacles, pushing them back against the bridge of his sharp nose, and went downstairs to breakfast. Mrs.

O'Toole hurried into the dining room with the plate of bacon and eggs she had been keeping in the warming oven, and poured his coffee.

"You're looking fine this morning, Mister Nider," Mrs. O'Toole said.

"You're looking fine yourself, Missus O'Toole." He winked at her as he spread his napkin across his lap. "Pretty as a picture."

She was big, raw-boned, and ugly, but she liked his flattery. She said—"Aw, go on with you now."—and fled into the kitchen. He laughed silently and began to eat, wondering what she would do when he brought Marian Tracey here as his wife.

This morning he couldn't keep his mind on Marian. He was too close to the fulfillment of a dream. He thought about the old days when Broken Nose consisted of his store on one side of the road and Chauncey Morts's saloon on the other, and when Old Mike Varney drifted into the country with his pretty wife twenty years younger than he was, two small children, a few cows, and an ambition that knew no legal or moral boundaries.

Broken Nose had grown and so had Old Mike Varney. Nider had immediately disliked him because he'd been an overbearing, aggressive bully from the day he'd started Pitchfork up there on Sundown Mesa. Within a year that dislike had turned to hate because Old Mike had shot and killed two men who were friends of Nider's. Fair fights, if you want to call them that, but the fact remained that the men were dead and Pitchfork absorbed their ranches. Old Mike was on his way.

Then there was this other thing. Clara Varney had been too good for an old bastard like Mike. Nider was reminded of a great, ugly bear holding an exquisitely delicate and beautiful doll in his hands. He was capable of smothering her to death, of tearing her apart, and, although he had never actually harmed her physically, he had smothered her and torn her apart in every other way.

Funny thing! Of all the women he had met and could have married, he had to pass them up and fall in love with a woman he couldn't have. He finished eating and settled back in his chair with a cigar. Thinking about how it had been, he couldn't actually put his finger on the moment he had fallen in love with her, but he did remember how he used to look forward to her coming into the store the way a child looks forward to Christmas.

She didn't come often. Sometimes she had the twins, sometimes not. When she didn't, she would linger at the dry-goods counter while he showed her every bolt of cloth on his shelves, and maybe the latest shipment of hats that had come in from Denver.

Maybe she bought a few yards of bombazine for a new dress or something for Vida, or possibly a hat, even if she didn't have any occasion to wear it. But that didn't matter. Far more important was the fact that both of them made the moments last as long as they could, usually until Old Mike left the Stockade across the street, reeking with Chauncey Morts's whiskey, stomped in, and demanded what in hell was keeping her.

That went on for several years until his want of her was a steady ache. Finally, when he couldn't stand it any longer, he said: "Come back into the office, Clara. I've got something I want to show you."

When she was inside, he shut the door and leaned against it. "It wasn't anything I wanted to show you," he said. "It was something I've got to tell you."

She knew before he said it. He remembered how she had trembled and how her face had turned white. She whispered: "Don't, Phil. Let it be the way it is."

"I can't. I've got to tell you. I love you and I think you love me. I've got some money and I can sell the store. I want you to go away with me. Bring the kids. I'll make you happy, Clara. I'll do anything for you. I'll take you anywhere you want to go."

Sentimental talk for an ex-train robber. Foolish talk, too, because in those days there was a reward out for him, and farther east there were a few Reward dodgers still floating around. The possibility that some observant sheriff would recognize him was a definite threat.

She didn't say no. She stood looking at him, trying to hold back the tears, her hands knotted at her sides. Then he went to her and took her hands. "You will, won't you, Clara? Give me a few days to get rid of the store."

"No," she said. "He'll kill you."

At the time he hadn't realized how much she was thinking of him. He said: "No, he won't. I'll kill him if it comes to that."

"No," she said again. "I made my choice when I married him. Now there's the children."

He put his arms around her and kissed her, and her arms flew around his neck and she returned his kiss. No other woman had ever kissed him like that; he had never felt again as he had at that moment. Even after all these years, he remembered how it was. He had sensed there was a smoldering fire in her that could be fanned into a high, bright flame, and, when he kissed her, he knew he had been right.

He still believed he could have talked her into going away with him if they hadn't heard Old Mike's bellow: "Clara! Where the hell are you?"

She jerked away from Nider and opened the door and walked out of the office, her head high and proud. She looked as guilty as sin. Nider knew he must have, too, but she carried it off. "Mister Nider was showing me a catalog he just received, Mike," she said. "There's a lace tablecloth I've just got to have. He can order it for me, can't he?"

"Sure, get it for her, Phil," Old Mike said. "Come on. Time to go."

"You get it for me as soon as you can, Mister Nider," Clara said, smiling sweetly, too sweetly, and left the store.

So he had to rustle around and get a lace tablecloth for her. After that it was never quite the same. She didn't linger at the dry-goods counter as she used to. She never came into the store unless Old Mike or the twins were with her. She was afraid of what would happen if they were alone, he thought, so she saw to it they never were.

He got up, suddenly restless, and, taking his derby hat off the rack in the hall, put it on and went outside into the morning sunshine. He glanced at the Flat Tops, made a little hazy by dust and the smoke from a distant forest fire. Pitchfork's summer range was up there. If the hot, dry weather continued, even it would dry up.

Early yet. Old Mike wouldn't be in town for a couple of hours, so Nider turned toward Marian Tracey's house at the end of the street. He had been a fool, he thought bitterly, or he would have killed Old Mike Varney years ago. Instead, he had foolishly hoped that someone else would do the job because Old Mike had made enemies right from the first.

If that had happened, Clara would have married him. He was sure of it. On the other hand, if he had killed her husband, she wouldn't have had him. He was sure of that, too, so he had let the years run by, and then Clara had died from typhoid and it had been too late.

After that he began to plan. He'd kept working on Charlie Gilbert every chance he had, reminding him that, if it wasn't for Old Mike, Charlie could have had a saloon here in town. When Turk Allen had put Sid Kehoe to bed with a beating, he'd gone to Wineglass and reminded Sid that Old Mike was too proud to turn down a gunfight, so Sid had sent for his brother Ace.

Old Mike would be taken care of later today. That left the twins, Vida who was so much like her father, and Bill who was some of both his parents. Nider walked slowly, realizing that his hate had become an obsession, but having no desire to fight it. Vida would marry Turk Allen and that would be punishment for her. Allen was a man who rode his reins instead of his horse; he was like that in everything and in time he'd break any woman he married.

Bill was another problem. He had much of his mother's gentleness and decency and pride, but he had his father's fighting qualities. Nider had expected the boy to leave home before this, and he wasn't quite sure why he hadn't. Sooner or later he would, if Old Mike lived, but now Old Mike was going to die, so Bill would stay, unless he tangled with Turk Allen. That seemed a good possibility, and the thought pleased Nider. But it would take time to bring it about. The immediate problem was to keep him from marrying Marian Tracey, and he was confident he could manage that.

Mrs. Tracey was in her rocking chair as usual. Nider turned through the gate and walked up the path, raising his hat to Mrs. Tracey when he reached the porch. Marian made a skimpy living for them, but if Nider stopped their credit at the store, they'd be on starvation rations.

Mrs. Tracey was fifty, but she looked seventy, claiming one pain after another until she had finally succeeded in reducing her activity to only three movements—to the rocking chair, to the table when Marian called that a meal was ready, or to bed.

"How are you this morning, Missus Tracey?" Nider asked.

"Oh, Mister Nider, I'm so glad you dropped by." She waved her fan languidly in front of her face with one liver-spotted hand, the other on her lap. "I saw the doctor again yesterday. I've had a bad pain, you know, for weeks, but I didn't say anything about it. I don't like to worry Marian. After suffering in silence all this time, I finally told her and she called Doctor Ripple." Mrs. Tracey swallowed, blinking fast so it gave the impression she was about to cry, even if she couldn't actually squeeze out a tear. "Mister Nider, I've got to have an operation."

"I'm terribly sorry, Missus Tracey." He patted her on the back as he fought a smile that threatened. The thought that she would suffer in silence was enough to make him smile. "Doctor Ripple is good. You'll be all right."

"But we can't afford it, Mister Nider. I just don't know what we'll do."

"The Lord will provide," he said piously. "You'll see." He hesitated for a proper moment, then asked: "Is Marian home?"

"Oh, yes. She'll be awfully glad to see you. Just go right in."

He walked past her into the front room. The house was small, with only two bedrooms, a combination kitchen and living room, and this room where Marian worked. Dress goods, several pieces of pattern, a sewing machine, scissors, needle, thread, pins—all scattered around the room or spread over the big cutting table, and a dressmaker's dummy by the window. Laziness was not a part of Marian Tracey, and he found this admirable as he did so many other qualities he had observed in her.

He crossed the room and stood for a moment in the doorway, looking at the girl's back as she leaned over the sink in the kitchen. She was blonde with blue eyes and curly hair that wasn't quite dark enough to be gold. She was a gentle-mannered girl, not as pretty as Clara had been when she'd first come to Pitchfork, but pretty enough, with a sweet-shaped mouth and a sharp little chin and dimples in both cheeks. She was by far the most attractive woman on Skull River. If the old lady would just drop dead and he could get rid of Bill Varney, he'd be fixed.

He said softly: "Marian."

She whirled from the sink, holding her wet hands high. "Phil, are you trying to scare me to death? I didn't know you were in the house."

"Your mother said just to come in." He crossed the room to her. "She says she needs an operation."

"I know." Marian turned back to her dishpan. "I guess she talked Doctor Ripple into it."

Only on rare occasions did she show a little irritation as she did now. Nider wanted to say that maybe the old lady would die under the doctor's knife, but he couldn't risk such levity with her.

"Marian, you've kept putting me off, but don't do it now," Nider said. "Marry me. Today. Tomorrow. Any time, and I promise you that your mother will get the best medical attention it's possible to give her."

Marian looked at him and shook her head. "I can't marry you on that basis, Phil. You're a good, good man, and you've helped us in so many ways, but I just can't saddle you with this."

He put an arm around her waist. "You're foolish. If you do need any help, I'll be here." He kissed her. She submitted, but she gave nothing back. She baffled him, refusing to send him away, but still not encouraging him, either. "I've got to go. Remember now."

"Thank you, Phil," she said softly.

He went out through the back door, not wanting to commiserate with Mrs. Tracey again. He walked slowly toward the store, wondering how Old Mike Varney would look when he was dead. Would his mustache still bristle, or would it collapse as a dead thing should? *It would bristle,* he thought with sudden savagery, *the damned thing would bristle until the old bastard rotted in the grave.*

Chapter Five

The Varneys and Turk Allen reached town shortly after 11:00. They reined up in front of Nider's store, and all except Bill dismounted. Old Mike's gaze involuntarily turned to the Stockade Saloon across the street. Ace Kehoe was probably there now, Bill thought, and Old Mike knew it. But he had until noon. He'd figure there wasn't any use dying until he had to. He always looked at things like this in the same cold-blooded, detached way.

Old Mike tied his horse, then stood motionlessly in the hot morning sunshine, opening and closing his right hand, then rubbing it up and down along his pants leg. Vida had been right about his rheumatism. He'd grunted and groaned all winter with it. He'd been to see Dr. Ripple, but nothing had brought relief except hot weather. Now, even with the pain gone, the stiffness remained in his wrist and fingers.

Old Mike was a realist above all other things, so he knew he had no chance against a gunslinger like Ace Kehoe. But chance or not, he wasn't ducking a fight. Bill hated his father's greed and ruthlessness and brutality, characteristics he did not understand. He did not understand, either, the cool disdain for death that had always been in Old Mike, but he admired it just as he admired his father's cow savvy and patience and foresight, qualities that had done more, in Bill's opinion, to make Pitchfork what it was than the greed and ruthlessness that people were inclined to remember.

Phil Nider came out of the store, calling: "Come in, Mike! The rest of you, too. No sense standing out here in the hot sun."

"Got that mower all hitched up and ready to go?" Old Mike asked.

"Well, it's ready to go," Nider said.

Nider must know what was coming, Bill thought, but he chose to ignore it just as Old Mike did. He was a queer one, this Phil Nider. Bill couldn't figure him out. He never got excited or lost his temper. Bill had never heard him curse; he had never known him to get drunk or fight a man or carry a gun. He had never even heard him laugh aloud.

You never knew what Nider was thinking. A cool smile, steel-rimmed spectacles astride a sharp nose, a distant manner that chilled familiarity—that was Phil Nider and you never got beyond or behind that exterior. Bill disliked the man, but honesty forced him to admit that his dislike was based on the fact that Nider was courting Marian Tracey and not on anything the man had said or done.

Turk Allen was watching Bill with close attention, frowning a little. *He doesn't think I'll go ahead with it,* Bill thought, *but he's hoping I will and he's hoping I'll get killed.* Vida was watching him, too, but he saw real concern in her face, and doubt as if she wasn't sure she had done right in asking Bill to pick up Old Mike's fight.

"I'll ride around to Marian's place and see if she's home," Bill said.

He thought that would strike flint in Nider, but the store-keeper acted as if he hadn't heard. So did Old Mike and Turk Allen. Vida said: "All right, Bill. We'll see you in the hotel dining room at noon."

He nodded and rode on down the street, thinking it was queer how all five of them could play this game out, ignoring

45

death as if it were vaguely distant instead of only minutes away. And it was death for someone, for him or Ace Kehoe, or Old Mike if he failed.

When he reached the end of the block, he glanced back and saw that all of them had gone inside. Instead of turning right toward the Tracey house, he swung left and reined into the alley. He followed it until he reached the loading platform behind the Stockade, then stepped down, and, leaving his horse ground-hitched, vaulted to the platform.

He checked his gun and eased it back into his holster, wishing he knew something about Ace Kehoe. He had seen plenty of gunfights and he had been in a couple, but they had been the results of quarrels that naturally come to a troubled range. Bill knew he was faster on the draw than most cowhands, but that proved exactly nothing because men who work cattle are seldom fast with their guns. Ace Kehoe was another kind of man.

For a moment Bill hesitated, seeing this in the cold light of reality. He had not lived close to a normal lifetime as his father had. He could not, and perhaps that was the reason, look upon death with the aloofness Old Mike apparently did.

Suddenly he thought of the many things he wanted to do and hadn't; he thought of his friends like Shaniko Red, of Marian Tracey, and with that thought came the certainty that he loved her. He had never admitted it before, yet he sensed he had known it all the time. He just hadn't been quite ready to recognize it, but he would tell her, he told himself, if he lived through this.

He took a look at the blue sky. He might never see it again. He swallowed and licked dry lips, feeling the prickle of sweat as it broke through every pore in his body, then he started toward the back door, threading his way through the beer barrels. He had gone too far to quit, and hesitation now would only lessen his chances of coming through this alive.

He crossed the storeroom and opened the door into the saloon. Chauncey Morts was behind the bar, his apron covering the bulge of his belly. He liked to say he was his own best customer, claiming that proved he served good beer.

There was only one man on the opposite side of the bar. Ordinarily, even on a weekday, there would be more than one patron here, so the story must have got around. The man glanced at Bill, and apparently made up his mind it wasn't Old Mike, for he immediately turned his gaze back to Chauncey Morts.

"So you're the old bastard's friend," the man said.

He'd be Ace Kehoe, Bill thought. He resembled his brother Sid, dark with a drooping mustache, a little on the skinny side with a fat nose that looked ridiculous on so thin a face. He carried his gun in a tied-down holster, a short-barreled gun that gave Bill the notion the man was fast, that he'd depend on speed rather than accuracy with his first shot. A lot of gunslingers were like that, he'd heard. Get close to the victim and figure that, if he threw enough lead before the other man fired, the odds were that one of his bullets would score a hit.

"Sure I'm Old Mike's friend," Chauncey Morts said.

"From what I've heard, I figured he didn't have any," Kehoe said.

"Then you're in for a hell of a surprise," the saloonman snapped, "and maybe a rope if you kill him."

Kehoe laughed unpleasantly. "I'll kill him, and even in a damned poor country like this, I don't reckon you hoist a man for killing a son-of-a-bitch like Old Mike Varney in a fair fight. Like I said, I don't figure he has a friend on Skull River."

"He's got a son whether he's got any friends or not," Bill said. "Fill your hand, Kehoe."

Surprised, the gunman wheeled from the bar to face Bill. He said to Morts: "This young Varney?"

"That's right," Morts said. "Looks like you'll never get a chance at Old Mike."

"The hell I won't," Kehoe said. "I made a long ride to get square for the beating my brother Sid got. My quarrel's with the old man, not the pup."

"You'll have to shoot the pup before you get a crack at the old wolf," Bill said. "I told you to fill your hand."

Bill had stopped at the end of the cherry-wood bar. Kehoe stood at the street end, so the entire length of the long bar was between them. Now it seemed to Bill that this distance between them was disturbing to the gunman.

Kehoe said, being careful not to move his right hand that was close to the butt of his gun: "Call the kid off, Morts. I tell you it's the old man I'm after. From what I'd heard, I didn't figure he was too yellow to do his own fighting."

"He doesn't know I'm here," Bill said. "I figure you're the yellow one, trying to rig a fight with an old man who's had rheumatism all winter and can't pull a gun in less than five seconds."

"That right, Morts?" Kehoe asked, not taking his eyes off Bill.

"Right as rain," Morts said. "Old Mike's so stove up I reckon the greenest kid in town could kill him. Won't be no credit to you."

Bill stood facing Kehoe, his weight forward on the balls of his feet, his right hand loose at his side. He was ready, but, if this lasted much longer, he'd tighten up, and suddenly it occurred to him that Kehoe was counting on that very thing happening.

"I'm done waiting," Bill said. "Make your play or I'll blow your god-damned head off with your gun still in leather."

Kehoe started moving toward Bill. "Stand where you are!" Bill yelled. "Don't try sneaking up on me!"

Kehoe stopped, his thin face tightening. He didn't like this, but apparently saw no way out of it. He swept his gun out of leather and fired.

Fast! The fastest draw Bill had ever seen, and, while he was frantically swinging his gun into line, the thought rushed through his mind that he was a dead man, that Ace Kehoe could trigger three bullets out of his gun before he could fire once.

Half of his thinking was right. Kehoe did get three shots off, the last one so close that it was a breath on Bill's left cheek. Then he felt the solid buck of the gun in his hand and gun flame was a bright blossom in the gloom of the saloon. The crashing roar of his gun seemed much louder than Kehoe's shots; the echo slammed back against his ears.

Kehoe spun around, his fourth shot the result of the involuntary twitch of his trigger finger. Bill's second bullet struck him as he started to fall, then Kehoe was face down in the sawdust, his hat coming off his head. Bill ran toward him, firing a third time before he realized the man was dead and it was finished and he was still alive.

He stood, staring down at the man. Then he slipped his gun back into his holster and put a hand against the bar. He heard Chauncey Morts: "Here, have a drink, boy. By God, that was good shooting. You sure kept your head. That'll teach 'em to send a gunslinger into this country."

Bill took the drink. He felt the jolt of it as it hit his stomach and he felt the warmth of it. Men began crowding in through the swinging doors. Sheriff Ed Grant. Dr. Ripple with his black bag. Phil Nider. Turk Allen. His father, and behind the old man he saw Vida, pale and scared and visibly relieved. Then Allen pushed her back through the batwings onto the sidewalk.

Dr. Ripple, past sixty with a white beard that made him look older, kneeled beside Kehoe. He got up a moment later, shaking his head at Old Mike. "Dead enough to stink before he hit the ground. Tote him over to my place, boys. They always wind up over there."

The sheriff walked to the bar. "How about it, Chauncey? You see it?"

The customary question. Morts said: "Sure I seen it. Kehoe pulled first. Bill had to shoot him."

Then the customary statement. "Justifiable homicide," Grant said. "I ain't holding you, Bill."

But Bill's gaze was on his father, straight-backed and furious, his faded eyes on fire the way they were when rage took hold of him. He paced slowly toward Bill, and, when he spoke, he laid his tongue on him the way he would have used a blacksnake in his hand.

"Who told you I'd got to the place where I couldn't do my own fighting?" Old Mike said. "Who told you you'd got big enough to walk in here . . . ?"

Bill turned and strode out through the back the way he'd come in. What was the use, he thought, and wondered if he had ever done anything right in his life in the eyes of Old Mike Varney.

CHAPTER SIX

Bill mounted and rode along the alley to Main Street and crossed it and went on. He was tired, deeply and physically tired. He had no regrets about killing Ace Kehoe. The man was a paid gunslinger and not a very brave one at that. He'd come here with the stated intention of killing an old man crippled up with rheumatism, a killing for which he would not have been held by the law, but which still would have been, by any moral standard, a clear case of murder.

No, Bill had no regrets about the shooting. If all the gunmen in the world like Kehoe went out the same way, the West would be a better place in which to live. He thought about Kehoe's brother Sid who was limping around his ranch, still bunged up after his fight with Turk Allen. He didn't even have guts enough to be in town the day Ace was supposed to kill Old Mike.

The beating was a typical Turk Allen job, and Bill would never have ordered it if he had been running Pitchfork. Still, he had no regrets about that, either, for Sid Kehoe was a furtive, belly-crawling kind of man who probably had done his share of rustling Pitchfork beef.

Maybe it was just that Bill had faced death and now found himself alive. He had built himself to an emotional peak to do the job, and it was over, so he was bound to feel a reaction. But he knew immediately that was not the full answer to why he felt the way he did. He had done this for his father, but Old Mike, instead of being grateful for having his life saved, had behaved in the typical Old Mike Varney manner.

Bill had hoped, more than he had consciously admitted, that what he had done would smooth things between him and his father, make it possible for him to change his mind about leaving. Instead, it had only widened the gap. He had been a fool for even hoping it would do anything else.

He wanted a little peace, a little quiet; he wanted to find a place where he could escape from the turmoil and the hate and fear Old Mike had kept alive in this country for the past twenty years. Without conscious thought, he turned toward Marian Tracey's house, knowing that was the only place where he would find what he sought.

He rode past Phil Nider's house, the show place of Broken Nose with its mansard roof, the metal fence, the bronze deer in the yard. Funny about Nider, he thought. A bachelor, he seemed to have no great desire for money, having been easy with credit as long as Bill could remember.

Still, Nider had prospered, and the talk was that he was better fixed than Dr. Ripple or the banker, Frank Burnham, or anyone else in Broken Nose. He could give Marian anything she wanted with none of the hard work and responsibility that would fall to her if she married Bill and went to live on Pitchfork.

Well, he'd see her and tell her good bye, and then ride to the ranch and pick up a few things and get the hell off Old Mike Varney's property. He could forget he had a father. Even forget he had a sister, for he was remembering it was Vida that had got him into this fight today.

Dismounting, he left his horse in front of the Tracey house and walked up the path. Mrs. Tracey was in her rocking chair on the front porch. She'd be there, he thought, or at the table, or in bed. If anyone deserved a golden crown, it was Marian for putting up with her mother.

Bill touched his hat to Mrs. Tracey. He said as courteously as

52

he could: "Howdy, ma'am. Marian home?"

Mrs. Tracey glowered, her skinny hands folded on her lap, her chair making a steady groan as she rocked. She was an old crow, he thought, who had worn herself out by her own nagging. She had no reason to love life, apparently gaining little satisfaction out of anything except the recitals of her ills, and yet she would be the last person in Broken Nose to welcome death.

"Young man," Mrs. Tracey said after a long silence, "do you have honest intentions toward my daughter?"

This was the last thing he expected to hear from her. Always before she had made it clear she didn't want Marian to marry. He didn't know what to say for a moment. Then he said lamely: "I don't have dishonorable intentions."

"That ain't what I mean," Mrs. Tracey said with asperity. "What I want to know is whether you have any intentions at all?"

He had no idea why she was talking this way. He was angry, but he didn't want to quarrel with her. Suddenly he realized that any man who married Marian would have to take her mother, too, and putting her out there on Pitchfork with Old Mike would raise hell and put a stick under it. Then he remembered he was leaving Pitchfork. He couldn't marry any girl, so why was he worrying about it?

"That's my business," he said curtly. "And Marian's. I asked if she was home."

Mrs. Tracey waggled a bony finger at him. "Mine, too, young man. Your father is wealthy, but I understand you're not. You work for wages the same as any other cowhand. Marian deserves more than you can give her, but for some crazy reason she likes you. As long as you keep hanging around, she won't say yes to Phil Nider, but, if you stayed away, she'd marry him. I'm not thinking about myself, you understand. Just Marian. Maybe you'd better start thinking about her, too."

He stared at Mrs. Tracey, hands clenched, fighting a desire to reach out and throttle her. She was lying. She was an old bitch who never thought about anybody but herself. Still, there was truth in what she'd just said. He'd had much the same thought as he'd ridden past Nider's house. He turned and started down the path to his horse, then wheeled around when he heard Marian's cry: "Bill, aren't you even going to see me?"

"Your mother wouldn't say whether you were home," Bill said.

Marian glanced at her mother, then back to Bill. She was silent for a few seconds, biting her lower lip as if she were struggling with her temper. Then she said: "Well, I am home. Come on in."

She held the screen open, motioning for him to go in. He walked past Mrs. Tracey who was rocking energetically now, her hands gripping the arms of her chair so hard that the bones threatened to break through the skin of her knuckles. She glared at Bill, making no effort to hide her dislike for him.

Marian was silent until they were in the kitchen. She closed the door and leaned against it, eyes searching Bill's face. She had a sweet-shaped mouth, and it seemed to him that her mouth was the key to her disposition.

She was quiet, steadfast, and gentle-mannered, and suddenly it occurred to him that she was much like his mother had been, somehow managing to find peace of mind in a life that held no peace, and, like his mother, deserving far more than she was receiving.

Impulsively he took her hands, forgetting that he couldn't take a wife because he was leaving and he would have no means to support her, no home to which he could take her.

He said: "Marian, I've never told you I loved you because I didn't know for sure until today. It hit me. . . ." He stopped, realizing he couldn't tell her about Ace Kehoe and that he hadn't been sure he loved her until he'd faced Kehoe's gun, so he said: "Well, it just hit me. That's all."

"I love you, too, Bill," she said softly. "I guess I wanted to hear you say that more than anything else in the world."

He kissed her, her arms around him, her body pressed against his, and for this moment he had the peace and quiet that he needed, the memory of Ace Kehoe and Old Mike and Turk Allen blotted out of his mind.

When she drew back to look at him, her hands on his shoulders, he blurted breathlessly: "Marry me. Today. I'll take you out to Pitchfork. You like Vida. You'll get along with her."

The shadow of worry was upon her face at once. She dropped her hands and, turning, crossed to the range and filled the firebox with wood. She faced him again, motioning toward the sofa at the other end of the room.

"Sit down, Bill. I was just getting dinner. You'll stay, won't you?"

"Glad to. But you didn't answer me. I want you to marry me. Or didn't you hear?"

"I heard. I've always thought I could say yes if you ever asked me. I want to marry you more than anything else in the world. You've got to believe that." She turned her back to him again and, lifting the lid from a steaming pan, looked into it. She replaced the lid and stood there, her back still to him. "But I can't, Bill. I just can't. You know why."

He crossed to her. "On account of Old Mike? He's sure hard to live with, any way you take him. Nobody gets along with him but Vida. And Turk who figures he's got to. But I thought maybe you could put up with him for a while. You wouldn't have much to do with him. Vida looks after him when he needs anything."

"It's not Old Mike."

"Well, I don't have much to offer you, if that's what you're thinking. You know how it's been on Pitchfork. I'm just a hired hand, but we'd have Vida on our side. We'd get along. Thirty dollars a month won't go far, but. . . ."

She turned to him, motioning for him to be silent. "It isn't that, either. You ought to know. Have I got to say it? Have I got to tell you what my mother's like when you saw for yourself a little while ago? I couldn't take her to Pitchfork and I couldn't leave her here. You couldn't come here to live with us, either. There isn't any way out for us, Bill. There just isn't any way."

He knew about her mother, all right, but he had forgotten about the old lady in his sudden anxiety to have everything right with Marian. He'd been stopped by his own problems, too, unable to think beyond them. Marian was right, of course. Suddenly he was reckless, wanting to disregard everything and everybody except Marian and him. They were young, they had a right to their future, to their happiness.

He brought her to him again and kissed her hard and brutally, letting her know and feel the need he had for her. When he let her go, he said: "Go off and leave her. Do something. There must be an answer."

"I can't leave her, Bill," she said. "I've thought about it more than once, and I've wanted to, but I can't. I love you, but love isn't enough. You don't just throw all your obligations out of the window because you love someone else. You haven't done it, and Old Mike isn't dependent on you like Ma is on me."

That was true. Mrs. Tracey didn't appreciate all the things Marian did for her, but she expected them. Old Mike didn't expect anything from Bill. Still, he had fought and risked his life to save his father's. Now, looking at Marian and seeing the misery that was in her face, he understood how she felt, the pressure that duty had put upon her.

He walked to the sofa and sat down. Marian said: "I shouldn't have kissed you. I shouldn't have told you I love you. There just isn't any way out and I've known it all the time, but I've never been able to make myself face it before."

He rolled a smoke, his fingers awkward with the brown paper. He sealed the cigarette and lit it, not looking at her.

"Women marry without love," Marian went on, "because there are other things that demand so much from them. Our bill at Nider's store gets bigger each month. Our rent has to be paid. I don't know how much we owe Doctor Ripple, but it's a lot. I'm afraid to ask. And I'm not even sure I can go on making the little money that I do. That dress out there is for Missus Burnham, but she's got a figure like a sack of wool and she's hard to please. But I've got to, Bill. If I don't, she'll see I lose every customer I have."

He should have known, but she'd never been one to talk about her troubles. Again he thought of his mother who had let everyone see a sunny face when she must have suffered torment that he had never suspected. He got up and, walking to the stove, threw the cigarette stub into it.

He said: "I won't give up, Marian. There's got to be an answer."

"There is an answer," she said dully, "but I won't like it. You won't, either. I'm going to marry Phil Nider."

He stared at her, unable to believe he had heard those words. But he had heard them and he knew she meant it. She was not one to joke about a thing like this. All her talk about loving him, but she couldn't wait.

He turned and walked out of the house, not even glancing at Mrs. Tracey, but the sound of her rocking chair reached him even as he stepped into the saddle.

CHAPTER SEVEN

When Bill reached Main Street, he saw that the Pitchfork horses were gone from in front of Nider's store. They weren't tied at the hitch pole in front of the hotel where Vida had said they would eat, so apparently Old Mike, Vida, and Turk Allen had left town.

Bill had dinner at the Chinaman's place at the end of Main Street, then stopped at the bank to withdraw his money, $49.25, a piddling amount for a man twenty-three years old whose father was the richest man on Skull River.

"Aiming to make an investment, Bill?" Frank Burnham asked in his jocular way.

Burnham was a roly-poly, careless man with an effervescent sense of humor. The only reason he had been able to keep his bank solvent all these years was because he leaned heavily on Old Mike Varney for advice. Mrs. Burnham ruled the Broken Nose social set with an iron hand, and she was put out with her husband because he didn't handle the local financial and political worlds the same way. Instead, he bowed to Old Mike, or Phil Nider if the question wasn't important enough for Old Mike to decide, and all of Mrs. Burnham's nagging, which was considerable, didn't remove the smile from her husband's lips.

"Yeah, an investment," Bill said. "One I should have made a long time ago."

He pocketed the money and left the bank, ignoring the question in Burnham's eyes. There'd be plenty of gossip, he thought, when the story got around that he'd pulled out. Folks all up and down the river would say he was crazy for throwing away half of Pitchfork. Maybe he was, not having the slightest notion where he'd go or what he'd do. But one thing was sure. He didn't give a damn what people thought or said. All he wanted was to leave town without having to talk to anyone, but he didn't move fast enough. Sheriff Ed Grant caught him before he reached his horse.

"Been looking all over for you, Bill," Grant said.

The sheriff was a slender man about forty. He had a family and a healthy desire to live, but he had not been a bad lawman. Like Frank Burnham, Ed Grant listened to Old Mike, so he got along.

Bill faced Grant, having no idea what he wanted unless it had to do with the killing of Ace Kehoe. He dropped his hand to the butt of his gun, telling himself he wasn't going to jail for that.

"Thought you weren't holding me for that shooting," Bill said.

"Hell, I'm not." Grant stepped off the walk and stood beside Bill. "I need some advice. Maybe you can give it."

"Not me," Bill said. "I don't know anything."

Grant gestured impatiently. "You know something about Old Mike, and he's the one I need advice about." He scratched a boot toe through the dirt, embarrassed because he wasn't quite sure how to say what he had in mind. Then he blurted: "Damn it, you know how it's been. If a man was gonna get anywhere in this country, he had to get along with Old Mike. I have, and I've never been sorry. Trouble is, he's long on telling the other fellow what to do, and stone deaf when it comes to listening."

If Bill hadn't felt the way he did, he would have laughed. The idea of Ed Grant or anyone else in town telling Old Mike what to do was something to laugh about. Bill said: "You ought to know better'n to try to tell him anything."

59

"But damn it, it's important. Maybe you can tell him. The business with Ace Kehoe today was just the beginning. They missed this time, but they'll try again. Sid Kehoe. The Gilberts. Phil Nider. It's been talk up to now, but. . . ."

"Wait a minute, Ed." Bill laid a hand on Grant's shoulder. "Did you say Phil Nider?"

Grant got red in the face. "I shouldn't have, I reckon. I mean, I don't know anything. Nider acts like a good friend of the old man's. He don't come right out and say anything. It's just that he's a cold fish and you never really know what he's thinking."

Bill dropped his hand. "No, I guess you don't."

"Well, leaving Nider out of it, there's plenty of trouble showing up with the others. I'm guessing again, but I figure from the talk I hear, and with Ace Kehoe dead, that the south side boys will show up some night when you don't figure on anything happening, and burn you out."

Bill shook his head. "You're dreaming, Ed."

"No, I ain't. Look at it this way. In the past twenty years the families north of the river have lost their spreads through one kind of pressure or another. Now Old Mike's got it all. So the boys on the south side figure they'll be next, but they ain't gonna wait to find out. You've got to put guards out and call some of your boys down from the Flat Tops."

"Old Mike wouldn't listen to you?"

"That's it in a nutshell," Grant said.

Bill stepped into the saddle. "He won't listen to me, either. Vida's the one for you to talk to."

Bill nodded at Grant, and, turning his horse into the street, rode out of town. He took his time, getting off his horse once and sitting on the riverbank for no reason except that he dreaded going home even for one more night. But he had to tell the old man, and he had to see Vida before he left.

Shaniko Red had said much the same thing Ed Grant had

just said. Well, Old Mike had been warned. If he wouldn't listen, he'd pay a high price for his bull-headedness. Bill didn't waste time worrying about that. He was more concerned about Grant's mentioning Phil Nider.

Maybe he should have argued with Marian, told her he'd get something better out of Old Mike, asked her to wait for him. With Vida's help, he might talk Old Mike into buying the house where Marian and her mother lived and letting them have it rent free. Maybe he could borrow enough from Frank Burnham to pay Nider's store bill. Pay Dr. Ripple, too.

So he had his dreams, smoking one cigarette after another, the sun dropping toward the broken country to the west, but in the end he was too practical to have any faith in the impossible. He would, he knew, get nothing from Old Mike.

On the other hand, there was Phil Nider who had waited patiently for Marian, Phil Nider who would give her all the comforts of life that she could ask for, Phil Nider who would see that Mrs. Tracey was taken care of the rest of her life. All that Bill Varney had to give Marian was his love, and she had frankly said that wasn't enough.

He got up, mounted, and rode home, a little sick with disappointment, knowing he had given Marian virtues she did not possess. Yet, weighing the hard realities she faced against the love he offered her, he found that he could not blame her. Then his thoughts returned to Nider and he wondered why Ed Grant had mentioned the man along with Sid Kehoe and the Gilberts, but he could think of nothing that satisfied him.

He reached Pitchfork just as the cook was beating the triangle for supper. He put his horse up, washed, and went into the cook shack. Turk Allen, who sat at the head of the long table, said nothing, but Shaniko Red, Birnie Hanks, and Dutch John had heard what had happened and congratulated him.

Allen went into the house as soon as the meal was over. Then the others had to hear Bill's account of the fight. Birnie Hanks was only twenty, a brash kid who hungered for trouble and frankly idolized Bill. Dutch John was in his late thirties, a heavy-set, stolid man who was an expert with his gun or his fists, but he was perfectly satisfied to earn his wages working cattle and let Birnie have the excitement.

When Bill told them what Ed Grant had said, young Hanks burst out: "Well, by God, we'll fix 'em! They'll sure as hell wish they'd stayed on their side of the river."

Dutch John snorted his contempt.

Shaniko Red said: "Five of us, Birnie. Six with the old man who ain't much on the shoot any more. There'll be a dozen of them. Maybe more. . . ."

"If Old Mike brings the boys down from the Flat Tops . . . ," Birnie began.

"He won't," Shaniko said flatly. "It's like Ed Grant told Bill. The old man talks but he doesn't listen."

Turk Allen came in, carrying a can of coal oil and several sticks wrapped with burlap. He said: "We're paying a visit to the Hell Hole." He looked at Bill. "You going?"

Bill hadn't intended to. He'd planned to go to the house as soon as the others left, say good bye to Vida, and tell Old Mike he was leaving. In the morning he'd be on his way. But he caught something in Turk Allen's eyes he didn't like, a sort of expectancy, as if a good deal depended on his decision.

If he didn't go, Allen would make something out of it. Hard to tell what he'd say to Old Mike. Maybe that Bill was yellow. Or he wasn't loyal to Pitchfork. Or that he'd been working hand and glove with the Gilberts. It didn't make much difference. Old Mike would swallow it whatever it was. "Sure I'll go," Bill said.

"All right." Allen turned to the others. "There'll be five of us. I've got jobs for all of you. Bill, you cut the pasture fence where the calves are. Shaniko, you'll turn the horses out of the corral. Birnie 'n' me will give you five minutes, then we'll hit the house and toss these torches on the roof." He nodded at Dutch John. "While we're doing that, you touch off the barn. We'll have a fire them bastards on the other side of the river will never forget."

Allen looked from one to the other, waiting for questions. It struck Bill that something was wrong. He couldn't quite put his finger on it, unless it was the uselessness of the job he'd been given. What was the sense of cutting the pasture fence? Probably all those calves had been stolen from Pitchfork, but nothing could be proved now. Ed Grant had been out there half a dozen times and he'd never found any evidence against Charlie Gilbert.

"Got it?" Allen asked. "I don't want no mix-ups. We won't get hurt if this goes off the way it's supposed to. Shaniko, you're the one who might get his tail in a crack. You split the breeze getting out of there soon as the horses are hightailing down the road. You're bound to make some noise. When Charlie and Lud hear it, they'll run out to see what it is. That's when we'll fire the house."

"One thing," Bill said. "I don't want Annie hurt."

Allen wheeled on him, no sign of his usual good nature on his face. "Who gives a damn about that floozy?"

"I do," Bill said. "She's a woman, whether she's a floozy or not. Just be sure she's not hurt."

"The old man didn't say anything about her," Allen said. "She'll take her chances same as the men."

Fury was a quick fire in Bill. This was like Old Mike, and it was like Turk Allen. Bill grabbed his arm. "I said you'll see Annie doesn't get hurt or you'll answer to me. Savvy?"

Allen jerked his arm free. "I'll answer to Old Mike, not his kid. You ain't 'rodding Pitchfork and I'd say it was a good bet you never will." He swung toward the door, calling: "Let's ride!"

It was dusk now. The air was still hot and heavy with the smell of dust and a forest fire from somewhere on the Flat Tops. By the time they reached the river, the darkness would be complete. As they crossed the yard to the corral, the thought was in Bill that none of this trouble was necessary. Retaliation, with one side striking and the other hitting back, would go on until one or the other was destroyed. This raid tonight would set it off.

Pitchfork had had its fights before, but none had been serious because the early victims north of the river had never been organized. The men to the south were. The fact that Ace Kehoe had come to Broken Nose seemed proof of that. Bill doubted that he would have come unless he'd been paid, and it was equally doubtful that Sid Kehoe would have ponied up all that money himself. A gunslinger didn't come cheap, even to a brother.

They saddled up and followed the wagon road to the rim—a grim and quiet party. They lined out in a single file as they rode down the shelf to the river, Allen in the lead. Twilight had given way to night, the last rose glow was fading in the west, the stars were coming out one by one dimly to light a dark world.

Old Mike had not given any real explanation for this raid. Not one that Bill had heard, anyway. Probably it was just that Charlie Gilbert was a market for Pitchfork calves and encouraged their theft. Regardless of who got hurt tonight, Old Mike would be beyond the reach of the law. Ed Grant would blandly say there was no proof that Pitchfork riders had made the raid.

Then, just as they reached the river, another thought came to Bill. Old Mike knew this business tonight would provoke a return raid. That was exactly what he wanted to happen. Then he would have the excuse he needed to move across the river.

CHAPTER EIGHT

Before they reached the upper corner of the calf pasture, Turk Allen stopped. Ahead of them were lit windows of Gilbert's house. There was no moon, so the night was as black as Allen could have wanted.

They waited for what might have been a minute, maybe two, and listened. No sound except the rush of the river to their left, the cry of some night bird farther downstream, and the whispering of the cottonwood leaves in the hot wind.

Allen said in a low tone: "Bill, you stay here. Give us several minutes, then ride on up to the pasture and cut the wire in three or four places. Birnie, stay with me. Shaniko, get them horses moving as soon as you can. John, start the barn to burning the minute the horses are in the open."

Bill remained, while the others rode on. He waited until he thought ample time had passed, then touched his horse, riding slowly until he was sure he had reached the pasture. Dismounting, he moved to the fence, his wire cutters in his hand.

He paused to listen, but could hear nothing except the faint sound of hoofs in the dust. He was uneasy, but didn't know why, unless it was his conviction that this was a damned fool play. It could turn into a death trap if there happened to be a bunch of Gilbert's friends in the Hell Hole.

A better way to play it would have been for the Pitchfork men to walk into the house, guns in their hands, and herd everybody outside, then fire the place. Old Mike had excuse enough, and he wasn't one to hide when he made a move like this, but he had left tonight's play up to Turk Allen, and a hit-and-run maneuver was typical of Allen's methods.

Bill cut the wires, listening to them snarl as they whipped back against the posts. A matter of seconds, no more, then Lud Gilbert's great voice rolled into the night: "Down here, boys, down here."

Young Gilbert wasn't far from Bill. The next instant he seemed very close, his gun sounding just as Bill swung into the saddle. Three shots, powder flame licking out into the darkness, the last bullet coming close. Bill had no time to think about how Lud happened to be there, no time to do anything except get moving.

He reined his horse around as other guns opened up farther down the road toward the house. Three or four. Maybe more. Bill didn't count them, but it seemed to him in those first frantic moments that the air was full of hornets, that gun flame was making twinkling orange ribbons all along this side of the pasture. He cracked steel to his horse and went rocketing back up the way he had come, riding low in the saddle, bullets still probing the darkness for him.

"After him!" Charlie Gilbert yelled. "He's getting away!"

They'd run him clear into town, Bill thought, if he didn't stop a slug between here and there. Suddenly he understood that strange expectancy in Turk Allen's eyes when he'd come into the cook shack with the torches and coal oil. Allen had set him up as a clay pigeon. Allen aimed to kill two birds with one stone—he'd draw the Gilberts away from the buildings and he'd get rid of Bill Varney who was in line to inherit half of Pitchfork.

Back at the Hell Hole firing burst out with sudden violence. That wasn't according to plan, but it probably saved Bill's life. Charlie Gilbert's voice rose above the gunfire: "Let him go!

They ain't after the calves! They're at the house!"

Bill pulled up and turned his horse. Hoofs were pounding back the other way. More firing. Annie Bain's frightened scream. Then a tongue of fire leaped up from behind the house. Dutch John had set the barn.

Bill had his gun in his hand, waiting, not sure what to do. Pitchfork had run into something Allen hadn't expected. The Gilberts had been warned about the raid and they'd been ready, along with some of their friends, but apparently they'd thought it was nothing more than an effort to steal the calves.

Hard to tell how much trouble the rest of them had run into. Bill stiffened, his senses alert. Someone was working toward him along the fence. A faint noise reached him during a lull in the shooting, of someone bellying through the grass.

He stepped out of the saddle and dropped flat into the road dust just as the man fired. He was closer than Bill had thought. If he'd stayed on his horse, he'd have got that slug through the brisket. He threw a shot at the gun flash, rolled toward the ditch at the side of the road, fired again, and spilled on into the ditch.

He hadn't missed. He was reasonably sure of that. He could hear the man's breathing and now and then a groan of pain. Again a burst of shooting from the house. Another fire. The house this time, Bill thought. He crawled forward along the bottom of the ditch, a few inches at a time, being careful to make no sound.

He heard the breathing again, and a groan, a few feet ahead of him. He found a rock and threw it, making a soft sound in the dust when it hit. Jumpy, the man fired at the noise, then Bill was on him, striking hard with the barrel of his gun.

He hit the man on the shoulder, forcing a yelp of pain out of him. He gripped his right arm, forcing it to one side, but barely far enough. The gun roared, the explosion so close it was deafening, the bullet burning a white-hot path along his ribs.

Bill struck with his gun barrel again, this time across the head, and the man went limp. Lighting a match, Bill held it close to the fellow's face. Whitey Matts, from the Lazy L. They'd been ready, damned good and ready.

Bill ran back to his horse and mounted. He was alone now, he thought. Whitey Matts had been left here to get him if he came back; the others had gone on. He rode toward the house that now was a bright, high torch. Shortly after he swung off the road into the sagebrush, a horseman loomed up ahead of him in the fringe of light from the fire. Bill raised his gun, calling: "Who is it?"

"Shaniko. Dutch John's around here, too."

Bill reined in. A moment later Shaniko pulled up beside him. The roof of the barn fell with a great explosion of sparks and uprushing flames, then subsided. The house fire had not yet attained its peak, the parched wood burning with a fierce crackling as the flames reached hungrily for the sky.

Heat touched Bill where he sat his saddle, coming in scorching, pulsating waves. He searched the yard, as bright as day in the red light, but he saw no sign of Annie Bain. He asked: "What happened to Annie? I heard her yell once."

"I got a glimpse of her right after she hollered," Shaniko said. "She was running toward the river. I figure she's all right." He sighed, his mournful face more melancholy than ever. "Sure a waste of good whiskey yonder."

"Where's Birnie and Turk?" Bill asked.

"Heading downriver the last I saw of 'em," Shaniko said. "I sure hope Birnie makes it."

Dutch John rode up. "Might as well go home," he said. "Old Mike's got what he wanted. Charlie Gilbert ain't gonna swap for no more Pitchfork calves."

"Maybe we ought to give Birnie and Turk a hand," Bill said.

"Naw," Dutch John grunted. "They had a good lead. Be easy enough to pull off somewhere and let the Gilberts ride by. Dark as it is, we might be shooting at the wrong bunch."

They swung back to the road, Shaniko asking: "How do you suppose that damned Turk worked it?"

"Worked what?" Dutch John asked.

"Got word to Charlie Gilbert. Hell, they was loaded for us. Plain as that big nose on your face. Turk aimed to throw one of us away. If Bill hadn't been along, I'm guessing it'd've been me cutting the wire."

"Who started the ball at the house?" Bill asked.

"Me," Shaniko answered. "I knew I wasn't supposed to, but I was just running the horses out of the corral when I heard the fireworks where you was. This thing didn't smell right to me from the start. I made a good guess what was happening when I heard the shooting, so I cracked a few caps to give 'em something else to think about."

"You sure saved my hide," Bill said. "I was heading for town all by my lonesome."

"Worked just the way Turk figured," Shaniko said, "except that you didn't get plugged. That bastard's got a coyote brain in his head. What are you gonna do about him when he shows up?"

"Nothing," Bill said. "I'm riding out in the morning. Old Mike can have him for a ramrod if he wants him. Vida can marry him, too."

"Hell, you've got to tell 'em what he done tonight," Shaniko said.

"Would they believe me?" Bill asked.

"No," Dutch John said. "Old Mike wouldn't, anyhow. I've worked for him longer'n you have, Shaniko, and I never knowed him to believe anything he didn't want to. But there's one thing about this deal I can't figure. Why did Charlie Gilbert have his men strung out along the pasture fence?"

"And why did he let us ride by without opening up?" Shaniko asked.

"He knew we were going to cut the fence," Bill said, "but he didn't know where. Maybe he figured we'd cut it in several places. As to why he let us ride by, my guess is it was too dark to tell for sure who we were. And knowing Ed Grant, he couldn't afford to open up till we made a move."

"Makes sense," Shaniko agreed.

They were silent until they reached the ranch, all of them made uneasy by their certainty that Turk Allen had intended for Bill to die tonight. He had never been liked by his crew. Now he would be hated. This was something for which he would never be forgiven.

When they dismounted, Bill said: "I'm going into the house."

"I'll take care of your horse," Dutch John said.

"Wait." Shaniko gripped Bill's arm. "I ain't leaving with you in the morning. You've got no business going now, neither. I don't give a damn about Old Mike, but I do about Vida. I'll kill Turk before I'll let him marry her."

They stood, staring at each other in the starlight, Bill knowing that Shaniko was right, but what his friend had said didn't change the way he felt. "I'll see," he said, and swung around and strode toward the house.

Vida was in the front room, restless and nervous, her face showing the strain she was under. She was plainly relieved when she saw Bill. She said: "I'm glad you're back. I've been worried." Old Mike was in his office, with the door open. She glanced at her father, biting her lip, then she asked: "Where's Turk?"

"He went one way with Birnie," Bill said. "Me 'n' Shaniko and John came this way." He touched her arm. "Vida, don't marry him."

She jerked away. "Do we have to go through that again?"

"He tried to kill me tonight. He's no good, Vida. I keep telling you, but you won't listen. Shaniko says if I don't take care of Turk, he will. Shaniko's been in love with you for a long time. He doesn't figure he's got any chance, but he knows what Turk will do to you, so he's not going to let it happen."

Her face turned fretful. She started to say something, then closed her mouth, and, walking to the leather couch, sat down. She had her pride and was a strong-minded woman. Bill could think of very few times when she had been able to back out of an untenable position. In that regard she was like Old Mike. She didn't ask how Turk had tried to kill Bill, and he realized that no amount of proof would convince her against her will.

When she remained silent, Bill said: "Whose job is it, your brother's or Shaniko who loves you?"

"Let him keep his love," she said, "and you stay out of my business. If Turk doesn't come back, I'll hold you responsible."

No use, Bill thought as he turned toward Old Mike's office. His mother must have felt exactly as he did now when she'd tried to stand against her husband. She had always failed just as Bill had failed every time he talked to Vida about Turk Allen.

Old Mike was working on his books when Bill came in, a cold cigar tucked into one corner of his mouth. He looked up, frowning. He said: "This is going to be a hell of a tough year. We've got to have more winter range, and, by God, I'll see we do, come winter."

No thanks for what happened in town today. No curiosity about what had happened at the Hell Hole. Not even an invitation to sit down. You play it out as long as you can, Bill thought. You keep swallowing your pride, hoping that something will happen to soften the old man, and all the time you know in your heart it never will.

"The Hell Hole's gone," Bill said. "Burned to the ground."

"Good," Old Mike said. "Now Charlie Gilbert can sell my

calves and get out of the country."

"He won't," Bill said. "You'll hear from him before long, him and Sid Kehoe and the rest. Ed Grant said he told you today."

Old Mike barked a laugh. "Yeah, he told me. He's an old woman. They won't do anything. Burn a little powder some night, maybe, and then you know what I'll do?" He tapped the blunt tips of his fingers against the desk top. "I'll have my winter range. Come fall I'll move my steers across the river. By spring every outfit on the other side will sell out to me and be gone, from Wineglass clean over to the Box H."

He started working on his ledger again, but Bill didn't take the hint and leave. He asked: "What does Phil Nider think of you?"

Old Mike reared back in his chair, chewing hard on his cigar. "Why do you ask?"

"Ed Grant named him today along with Sid Kehoe and the Gilberts. When I pinned him down, he couldn't tell me why. Just a hunch, I guess."

"More'n that," Old Mike said dourly. "Nider's a slick bastard, bowing and scraping in front of you and ready to stick a knife in your back all the time. I knew he'd come into the open one of these times. I figured it'd happen before this."

"Why?"

Old Mike tongued the cigar to the other side of his mouth. "Ed Grant knows. He just didn't want to tell you. All the old-timers know, though they've always been mighty careful not to let me hear any of their damned gossip." He jammed the cigar into the other side of his mouth again. "Phil Nider was in love with your mother. She thought she was in love with him, but I wouldn't let her go. I never give up anything that belongs to me. I told her I'd run 'em down if she left with Nider and I'd kill the son-of-a-bitch right in front of her."

He slammed a great fist down on the desk, his mustache

bristling with his temper. "Always walked soft and easy in front of me, Nider has. Done me good to see it, too, knowing how he hated all of us. I kept trading at his store. I let him stay in town. He knows I could finish him tomorrow if I wanted to. He figured I'd cash in and he'd get your mother, but, by God, he didn't."

Now, staring at his father's weather-lined, bitter face, Bill hated him as he had never hated him before. To all practical purposes, Old Mike had said he was glad his wife had died when she had so Phil Nider couldn't have her.

"You're giving up one thing that belonged to you," Bill said.

"What?"

Temper was a bright shine in the old man's faded eyes, the hard, brutal temper that over the years had made him what he was. Bill said: "Me. I'm leaving in the morning."

If Old Mike was surprised, he didn't show it. He asked: "Why? You've got a job here."

"If you don't know, I couldn't explain it," Bill said, and turned to the door.

"Wait," Old Mike said. "Better get this clear now. You walk out in the morning, and by night my will's gonna be changed. You've always been too soft. Too much of your mother in you. I've raised you the way I have to make something out of you. I aimed to make you man enough to hold on to what I'm leaving you. You've got no kick coming. Not any damned bit."

Bill stood motionlessly, watching his father and wondering how he could have been sired by this man. He said: "I'm not going to argue with you. I'm leaving."

"Then don't come back," Old Mike said. "Vida's got the right stuff in her. She'll hang onto Pitchfork, her and Turk. They're better off without you."

Bill walked out. Vida was on the porch, staring across the dark mesa. When Bill passed her, she said: "Have breakfast with us in the morning?"

"No," he said. "Old Mike would have indigestion if I did. So would I."

He went on past her to the bunkhouse. He said to Shaniko: "You look out for 'em if that's what you've got to do. Take care of 'em, and, when I see you twenty years from now, remember to tell me how much thanks you got."

After the lamp was out, he found that he could not sleep. He had not known about his mother and Phil Nider. He had never even suspected. He could not blame his mother. Maybe Nider wouldn't have been good for her, but it probably would have been better than living on Pitchfork with Old Mike. Anything would have been better than that.

Then he wondered if Nider really loved Marian, or was it his way of striking at one of the Varneys? Did Nider hate all of them that much? Old Mike intimated that he did.

Bill wondered, too, if Nider was the one who had passed the word to Charlie Gilbert about the raid, if Turk Allen had mentioned it in the store. *It could have been that way,* he thought, *it could have been.*

CHAPTER NINE

Phil Nider was the most surprised man in Broken Nose when he saw Ace Kehoe lying on the Stockade floor and Bill Varney standing there. All that shooting and young Varney not even touched. Ace Kehoe with his big reputation. It had taken $500 to bring him here. He wouldn't come just because his brother needed him. Money talked, he'd said. Well, it had talked and he'd listened, and now he was as dead as he'd ever be.

But Nider didn't show his surprise. He listened to Old Mike tear into Bill and he saw Bill walk out. He watched some of the men carry Kehoe's body to Dr. Ripple's back room. He watched Old Mike stalk across the street and ride out of town, his head held high and proud, with Vida and Turk Allen following.

Knots of townsmen had formed along the street. They talked about what had happened in low tones as if afraid Old Mike would hear them, even though he was well out of town by now. That was typical, Nider thought bitterly. The bastard could be ten miles away, but his shadow still lay over the town.

Nider started toward his store, then stopped when Frank Burnham called: "How do you figure it, Phil?"

"Figure what?"

"Bill taking the play away from his dad, and Old Mike getting sore about it. That's gratitude, now isn't it?"

"Ever see Old Mike show gratitude?" Nider asked harshly, and was instantly sorry he'd given that much hint of his feelings in his voice. He added in his usual mild tone: "Struck me that

Old Mike wanted to die and Bill had cheated him out of it."

Burnham, his face unusually grave, said: "No, I don't think Old Mike wanted to die. Of course, you're right about him never showing gratitude, but to cuss Bill out that way. . . ."

His voice trailed off as if uncertain about the whole business. Or maybe, Nider thought, he was afraid Old Mike would hear he'd been critical.

"You know how he is about having anyone else do things for him," Nider said. "I guess he didn't want to be beholden even to Bill."

"Yeah, I expect that's it," Burnham said.

Nider went on into the store and walked to his office in the rear of the long room. He shut the door, thinking as he often did that it was in this very room he had kissed Clara Varney, and that, if Old Mike had stayed in the Stockade just five more minutes, he'd have talked Clara into leaving with him. He had persuaded himself long ago that he could have done it, and now he didn't doubt it at all.

So he blamed Old Mike for the fact that he'd never had Clara, for all these lonely years while he had waited for the son-of-a-bitch to die, and now, after carefully shaping up this deal with Ace Kehoe and succeeding in staying out of the picture, Old Mike was still alive.

He was so lost in his thoughts that time slipped past. He was surprised when Carl Akins tapped on his door. Nider opened it, saying: "Well?"

"You didn't go home for dinner," Akins said hesitantly. "It's after twelve. If you ain't going, maybe it'd be all right if I. . . ."

"Sure," Nider said. "You go and hurry back. I'm going to be gone this afternoon."

"I'll hurry," Akins said, and left the store on the run.

Nider enjoyed his silent laugh as he watched his clerk go. Funny how people were afraid of their shadows. If Akins wasn't afraid of so many things, he'd go far. He was dependable, he worked hard, and he was so honest it was pitiful. He was the best clerk Nider had ever had, and he'd have doubled the man's pay if that was necessary to keep him, but still Akins was afraid he'd lose his job.

Even Frank Burnham in the bank was the same. He was caught between his wife on one side, and Old Mike on the other. Sometimes he was even afraid of Phil Nider, and Nider laughed again as that thought struck him.

Why, Marian Tracey was the same, afraid she'd make a mistake with Mrs. Burnham's dress goods, and, if she made Mrs. Burnham mad, she'd lose all her business. Afraid of her mother's nagging. Well, she had a right to be afraid of that. It was hell in big doses to have to listen to the old lady's complaints day after day.

Once he and Marian were married, he'd kill the old bitch. He'd thought about it many times. Or better yet, as soon as Marian promised him. She was the kind who wouldn't break a promise, once she'd made it. Spending a honeymoon in the Tracey house or even in his own with Mrs. Tracey still alive was an intolerable prospect.

Nider walked aimlessly around the store, busy only with his thoughts. He was honest enough to admit that this business of fear was one of the things that set Old Mike Varney apart from everyone else. He wasn't afraid of anything, not even of death. In that regard, his children were exactly like him. Well, Nider could admire the Varneys for their courage and still hate them.

Carl Akins must have gulped his dinner, for he was back in a few minutes and Nider left. When he reached the front of his house, he saw that Bill Varney was just leaving the Tracey place. Nider didn't break his stride, but turned through the gate to his metal fence and went up the path to the house.

He hated to think about what had gone on between Marian

and young Varney. He was comforted by the thought that not very much could go on with the old lady on the front porch. Bill might have kissed Marian and held her in his arms, but even that was too much. First Clara, with Old Mike standing between them, and now Marian and Old Mike's son.

He wouldn't lose a second time. He'd kill Old Mike and he'd kill Bill if he had to. He'd play on Marian's fear and he'd use Marian's mother as long as he needed her. No, it was going to be different this time.

He hung his hat on the hall rack and went into the dining room. "You're late, Mister Nider," Mrs. O'Toole called. "I'm afraid your dinner's spoiled."

"Then I'm to blame, Missus O'Toole," he said. "Have I ever blamed you for anything?"

"You never have." Mrs. O'Toole set a bowl of soup before him. "I'm not complaining. I don't mind when you're late." She started toward the kitchen door, then turned back. "I never have anything to complain about, Mister Nider. You're the best man in the world to work for."

She turned again and went into the kitchen. He scowled at his soup. Hell, she was afraid of losing her job, too. Just like Carl Akins. And Frank Burnham and the rest. It bothered him because he had always thought Mrs. O'Toole was made of better stuff than the rest of the townspeople.

There had to be courage somewhere. It took courage to fight a man like Old Mike Varney. But where? He wouldn't find it among the ranchers south of the river. Not unless they were properly led and organized, and all their fears and resentments fired into a destructive blaze. He could do it, he thought, but it meant coming into the open.

He considered this as he ate. He rated his brains and courage the highest in the country, but he liked the sly game, played from the wings and never on the stage in sight of the audience.

Putting little obstacles in front of Old Mike when he could, working on Old Mike's enemies in the roundabout way he had used with Sid Kehoe.

But in the back of his mind he had known that someday he'd have to come into the open, and by the time he had finished his pie, he had made up his mind. This was the time. If he worked it right, he would have the pleasure of personally killing Old Mike Varney.

He rose, calling: "I'll be late for supper, Missus O'Toole!"

"That's all right," she said. "I'll have something hot for you."

He got his hat, and, going back to the barn behind the house, saddled his bay gelding and left town, traveling downriver. There were two things he must do. The first was to see Charlie Gilbert, so he kept on the county road, following the river to the Hell Hole.

He had no affection or even respect for Charlie Gilbert. The man was a bull, filled with fire and fury, and if once he was forced into action, he would be hard to handle, or even turn into the right direction. He was nothing like Pete Matts of the Lazy L or Sid Kehoe of Wineglass or any of the ranchers south of the river.

Besides, the Hell Hole was a patch of perdition in an otherwise decent country. He had agreed with Old Mike in keeping Gilbert out of Broken Nose, but he had never stated his views, so Gilbert didn't know how he felt. The man could be used, and this was the time to start.

He found both Charlie and Lud working in a hay field along the river above the pasture that held the calves. Charlie was glad enough to take a breather, and he came to the fence when Nider called, wiping his round face with a bandanna.

"Hotter'n hell, ain't it, Mister Nider?" Charlie said.

"I suppose it is," Nider agreed, "but you don't know how hot hell is. Might be pretty warm down there."

Charlie laughed. "I reckon it is, all right, but I've got some notion what hell's like." He told Nider about the fight with Bill Varney and Shaniko Red.

"I didn't know about that," Nider said, "but I did hear something else that's part of the same thing. I thought you ought to know. The Pitchfork outfit is figuring on stealing your calves tonight."

Charlie blinked, his moon-like face showing doubt. "How do you know?"

"It's no secret how you operate," Nider said bluntly, "and it's no secret what Old Mike thinks of you and your operation. He's said more'n once he's going to run you out of the country and I'd say this was his way of starting."

"I asked how you knew."

"Turk Allen dropped a remark in the store," Nider said. "I was trying to sell Old Mike a mower I just got in. Turk said they'd need some new mowers next year because they'd be cutting hay down here on the river. Then he said they were starting on you by cutting your fence and stealing your calves back."

Charlie Gilbert was a suspicious man by nature, and now Nider saw the suspicion crawl into his face. He said: "You're a town man, Mister Nider. You stand with Ed Grant and Frank Burnham and the rest, and you suck around after Varney the same as the others. Could be Turk Allen wanted us to hear this."

"Why?"

"I don't rightly know," Charlie said thoughtfully, "unless it was to scare us."

"I think everybody in this country knows you don't scare," Nider said, "or you wouldn't still be here. You said one thing I want to correct. I don't stand with Ed Grant and Frank Burnham and the rest, and I don't suck around after Old Mike Varney. You've been in this country a year. I've been here twenty years. I've seen Varney build Pitchfork from an outfit the size of Wineglass or the Lazy L to the biggest spread anywhere on Skull River. I guess you know the methods he's used the same as I do. Well, he's ready to make another big move, and you know which way he'll come. I figure he's got to be stopped and he can't be if we don't work together."

Suspicion was still in Charlie's eyes. "You never talked this way before."

Nider tipped his derby a little forward on his head. He said: "I know I haven't, and I've been wrong. I've known for a long time that we had to do it, but I kept putting it off. Today I made up my mind. We can't put it off any longer. Every time a small ranch is sucked into Old Mike's hands, I lose business. If I have to get out and fight him myself to save my store, I'll do it."

"You're purty damned late," Charlie said truculently. "You've sat here twenty years. Now you want to fight. Why?"

"Well, it was just that I kept thinking somebody who had as many enemies as Old Mike has would get what he had coming and I wouldn't have to do it. You know what Turk Allen did to Sid Kehoe. They sent for his brother. I guess you put up some of the money it took to get him here. Today Bill Varney shot and killed Ace. That showed me something. If we want this job done, we'll have to do it ourselves."

Nider started to turn his horse, then stopped. "I came here to do you a favor. Maybe Turk Allen was just talking. I don't know, but I do know you're too smart a man not to be ready if they come cutting your fence and taking your calves. You've got quite a piece of money invested in them. I'd suggest you get a little help, too."

Nider rode away then, satisfied he'd said enough. He crossed the river, climbed to the south mesa, then turned east toward Wineglass. Turk Allen might have had his reasons for telling him what he had. Maybe he wanted Charlie Gilbert to hear it.

If Allen had stayed in town, he might have mentioned it in several places to be sure Gilbert knew, but after the shooting he'd left with Old Mike and Vida.

Turk Allen was a brutal and ruthless man like Old Mike, but he had a streak of craftiness, too, that the old man didn't have. Nider recognized this in others because he had the same kind of streak himself, but even by putting himself in Allen's place, he couldn't quite figure out what the man had to gain by permitting Gilbert to know Pitchfork's plans. But it didn't make any difference. A fight at the Hell Hole would be a good thing either way because it would precipitate action, and, if Nider was going to have allies, he had to have action.

Reining up, he looked across the valley at Sundown Mesa. He couldn't see the Pitchfork buildings, but he knew where they were and what they were like. He admired success in a man, even in Old Mike Varney. With Old Mike gone, what would happen? Bill would certainly leave after what had happened today. Vida and Turk Allen would be there, but Allen, for all of his slyness and brutality, was not the man Old Mike was.

Now it occurred to Nider that it would be fitting if, in time, he owned Pitchfork. If Clara knew what was going on, she'd like that, he thought. He knew a little bit about the cattle business, enough to run a ranch with the proper kind of help, and he could always get the help. He jogged on toward Wineglass, pleased with his thinking.

He told Sid Kehoe what had happened, suggested that this was the time to fight, and offered to help in any way he could. He rode home, getting there at dusk, and ate the warm supper Mrs. O'Toole had promised.

For a time he sat on the porch, smoking a cigar and reviewing the day's events, the early disappointment over Ace Kehoe's failure giving way to satisfaction. If you were going to succeed in anything, you had to keep working at it. He had taken his stand today and he felt good about that. He had tiptoed around far too long. In the morning he would start carrying the pearl-handled gun he kept in the bureau. The good people of Broken Nose had much to learn about Phil Nider, even after twenty years of living in the same town with him.

When he went to bed, he fell asleep at once, content with himself and the future. Shortly after midnight, he was awakened by someone pounding on his door. Irritated, he got up, put on his robe and slippers, and lit a lamp. When he opened the door, he was surprised to see Lud Gilbert standing there.

"Come in," he said, and stepped aside for Gilbert to enter.

Lud shook his head. "I ain't got time to come in. Pa, he wanted you to know what happened. They cut our fence, all right, but we was waiting for 'em. They didn't get no calves, but they burned us out. We ain't got nothing left."

Nider stood motionlessly, holding the lamp, too shocked for a moment to realize the full significance of this. Then he asked: "Where is your father?"

"In Doc Ripple's office. He got a slug in his left arm."

"Anybody else hurt?"

"Whitey Matts."

Lud started to turn. Nider asked: "What are you going to do?"

"Do? I'm going out there to Pitchfork and I'm gonna shoot that old bastard. We've been kicked around too many times."

"Don't do that," Nider said. "There's too many of them. They'll kill you and nothing will be gained."

"Maybe you've got a better idea," Lud said.

"I have," Nider said. "Wait and get Old Mike by himself. He always rides around in the daytime, usually alone, or maybe with his girl. You go up and hide in that old stone cabin north of the buildings. Sooner or later he'll show up. You can get him without getting killed yourself. Then maybe we'll have some peace on this range."

Lud stared at Nider with the same stubborn suspicion his father had shown that afternoon. "What good is this gonna do you?"

"It'll get rid of Old Mike," Nider said. "I told your father how it was with me this afternoon."

"Yeah," Lud said. "He told me." He licked his lips, finding it hard to change his slow mind. Finally he said: "All right, I reckon that would be a better scheme."

After Lud left, Nider dressed. Here was the situation he had been hoping would come about. Now the years of waiting didn't seem wasted or quite so foolish. He took his rifle and left the house, moving with care so he wouldn't waken Mrs. O'Toole. He saddled his horse and left town, but this time he didn't follow the county road. He headed directly for Sundown Mesa.

CHAPTER TEN

Bill ate breakfast with Shaniko Red and Dutch John, then drifted across the yard with them and watched while they saddled up. Neither Turk Allen nor Birnie Hanks had ridden in during the night. Bill was uneasy about Birnie, but he frankly hoped Turk Allen had been shot and killed by the Gilberts. If it had happened, he would have considered it an act of Divine Providence designed to save Vida.

Dutch John shook hands with Bill and stepped into the saddle. Shaniko Red hesitated, his forlorn face more melancholy than ever. He said: "Well, damn it, Bill, I reckon you think. . . ."

"No, I don't think anything of the kind," Bill said. "We've both got to do what we've got to do and that's all there is to it."

"This wouldn't be happening if some folks would just use a little horse sense," Shaniko grumbled, staring at the house. "If Vida could see. . . ."

"A woman doesn't use horse sense if she's in love," Bill said, "or thinks she is, and you never knew Dad to use horse sense when it goes against his grain."

"You wonder how he ever piled it up like he done," Shaniko said.

Bill gave him a tight grin. "When it comes to making a little *dinero,* he's not so bull-headed it hurts him any."

Shaniko nodded agreement. "Well, if Turk got his last night, I won't hang around here. You know where you're heading?"

Bill shook his head. "I'm going down Skull River into Utah,

then drift south. Pick up a job if I can find one. If I don't, I'll go on to Moab. Windy Reese is down there. Used to ride for us. You remember him?"

"Sure, you couldn't forget Windy." Shaniko held out his hand. "Well, good luck. Keep your neck out of a rope."

"I aim to," Bill said, and shook hands.

Shaniko mounted and rode away with Dutch John. Watching them, Bill had his doubts. There was always a fork in the road ahead of a man, he thought, and you had to make a choice. Well, right or wrong, he'd made his. It took him away from Shaniko and Dutch John and the rest who were his friends; it took him away from Vida, and, worst of all, he was surrendering Marian Tracey to Phil Nider without even making a fight of it.

He glanced toward the house, hoping Old Mike would come out and say: "Don't go. You're my son. I need you. Stay here with me." But it was still early, and the sun was throwing a long shadow behind him. Old Mike didn't get up at dawn as he used to. Vida would still be in bed, too, unless she was watching for Turk Allen to ride in.

It didn't make any difference whether it was early morning or noon. Not really. Vida was too worried about Turk to think of her brother, and Old Mike just didn't give a damn. Any hope Bill had of his father stopping him was a dream and nothing more.

He went back to the bunkhouse. He needed a pack horse, but the only animal he owned was his saddle horse. He didn't own much else, as far as that went. His saddle, his Winchester, his handgun, his clothes, and the $49.25 he'd taken out of the bank yesterday. That was the size of it. He guessed he didn't need a pack horse, after all.

Finding a flour sack, he stuffed his shaving gear and a few odds and ends into it. *Talk about your thirty years' gatherings*, he thought ruefully. Any drifting cowboy owned more than he did.

He straightened up and looked around, a dull ache inside him, a strange, poignant feeling he had not had since his mother's death.

He had spent a good part of his life in this room with the rest of Pitchfork's hands. Hired hands, he thought bitterly, and he'd been one of them.

Even Charlie Gilbert, a bad one by the ordinary standards, loved his boy Lud and needed him. Maybe he couldn't expect Old Mike to love anything except himself and Vida and Pitchfork, but at least his father could have looked upon him a little differently than he had the other men who drew Pitchfork wages. It was that lack of need, Bill thought in a sudden moment of clarity, that was driving him away more than anything.

He left the bunkhouse and crossed the sun-drenched yard to the corral where he roped and saddled his horse. He slipped his Winchester into the boot, and wrapped the flour sack in his slicker and tied it behind the saddle. He would have mounted then and ridden away if he hadn't looked up and seen Old Mike coming toward him from the house.

Leaving the reins dangling, he moved to the horse trough and took a drink out of the pipe that carried a constant flow from the spring above the house. He wiped his mouth on his sleeve and waited, angry with himself because a sudden flare of hope had rushed through him. One look at his father's dark, bleak face told him nothing had changed and nothing would change.

"Don't leave without seeing Vida," Old Mike said as he came up. "She fixed a sack of grub for you."

Bill said—"All right."—and waited.

Old Mike scratched the back of his neck, staring westward at Nevada Mesa. "Turk must have got into trouble last night," he said. "How do you figure it?"

A crazy, unreasoning rage took hold of Bill. Old Mike didn't give a damn about his own son, but he was some worried about his foreman. "I hope he got plugged," Bill said furiously. "He tried to set me up for a clay pigeon last night. What about Birnie? Maybe you better worry about him a little."

Old Mike gave him an oblique glance. "I'm thinking about Vida. She didn't go to bed all night."

"Who sold her on marrying Turk?" Bill demanded. "Was it because she's in love with Turk? Or because you want a man like him to run Pitchfork the way you've run it for twenty years?"

"Maybe both," Old Mike said. "You going to make a fight out of it the morning you leave?"

"If Turk was here, I would," Bill said, "but not with you. You never saw anything you didn't want to see, and you sure can't see through him. I figure Turk will show up after I'm gone. He won't come around till he finds out I'm dead. Or gone."

As Bill swung around toward his horse, he saw Birnie Hanks riding in from the west. He was alone. Bill paused, wondering if Turk Allen was dead. Probably not, he decided. Chances were Turk and Birnie had holed up in the line cabin on Nevada Mesa, and Turk had sent Birnie on ahead to find out what had happened to Bill, Shaniko, and Dutch John.

He stood with his back to Old Mike, watching Birnie, when he heard the rifle crack. As he wheeled, he realized the shot had come from the top of the ridge. The wild thought struck him that Turk was up there, trying to kill Old Mike so it would be laid onto one of the Gilberts or Sid Kehoe.

Old Mike was down on the other side of the horse trough. Another shot knocked a heel off one of his boots. Bill grabbed him by the shoulders and dragged him behind the trough as a third bullet kicked up dust inches behind him. Then Bill had the old man behind the trough and the shooting stopped.

The trough was full of water, giving adequate protection from the ridge top. Bill lay flat beside his father, his legs in the mud at the other end of the trough where the water flowed over the top and trickled across the yard.

Old Mike had been hit in the chest, but it was to one side and not necessarily a fatal wound. Bill wadded up his bandanna and, opening his father's shirt, laid it over the bullet hole that wasn't bleeding as much as he expected.

"Got to get you into the house and go after Doc Ripple," Bill said.

"Don't move," Old Mike said hoarsely. "You show your noggin over the top of the trough and you'll get your head blowed off."

That was probably true, but he couldn't lie here all day. The dry gulcher up there on the ridge could. He heard Vida scream from the front of the house, "Dad? Bill? You hurt?"

"Dad's hit!" Bill called. "Stay there."

Silence then, a tight silence that seemed to ribbon on and on without end, each second drawn taut until it seemed a full minute. For the first time in his life, Bill Varney was in a tight spot where he had to do something and couldn't do anything. But he wasn't going to stay here.

"I'll make a run for my horse," Bill said. "I'm going up after him."

"No, damn it," Old Mike said. "That slug's had my name on it for years, but it's different with you. Stay here."

"I can't," Bill said. "We'll be pinned here all day if I don't run him off that ridge."

He sprinted for his horse, expecting to feel the white-hot slice of a bullet, expecting to hear a shot. But he reached his horse and swung into the saddle, his gaze sweeping the ridge. He swore in surprise. For a moment he had completely forgotten Birnie Hanks. Now he saw that the boy was riding up the ridge. Crazy as hell, but the boy had guts.

"Birnie!" Bill yelled. "Birnie! Let him go! Come here!"

Bill dismounted, motioning for Vida to come to him. If the dry gulcher was still up there, he'd have cut Birnie out of his saddle before now. It sure wasn't Turk Allen, either, or Birnie wouldn't have headed for the ridge the way he had.

Bill ran back to his father. Vida was there, motionless, her face pale, plainly not knowing what to do. Birnie, Bill saw, was coming back down the ridge.

"We've got to get him into the house," Bill said. "Birnie can go for the doctor."

He picked up his father's limp body and carried him into the house. The old man was unconscious, probably from shock, Bill thought. He laid him on the bed, noting that the bullet had gone on through.

"Not a bad wound," Bill said, "but you never know. Get his shirt off and bandage him. If Doc's in town, it won't take Birnie long to fetch him."

He whirled toward the door, and Vida cried: "Where are you going?"

"I'm going after that killing bastard," Bill said, and ran out of the house.

Birnie was in the yard by the time Bill reached his horse. "Go get Doc Ripple," Bill said. "Bust the breeze. Old Mike's alive. He's got a chance."

Birnie asked: "Who do you figure it was?"

"I don't know. Where's Turk?"

"Yonder." Birnie grinned as he nodded toward Nevada Mesa. "Sent me to find out what happened last night."

He'd made a good guess about Turk's reason for not showing up, Bill thought, and jerked a hand at Birnie. "Get moving," he said, and, mounting, started up the ridge.

CHAPTER ELEVEN

Bill lost valuable time on the ridge hunting for the spot where the dry gulcher had waited. There had been no rain for weeks, so the ground, baked hard by the hammering sun, held few hoof prints except in the protected places where the wind had not blown the dust away.

No one was in sight north of the ridge, so Bill didn't have the slightest idea what way his man had gone. There was a chance Shaniko Red and Dutch John had seen him, but Bill couldn't count on that. Sundown Mesa was big. The fugitive might ride north for miles, turning east toward the county road that led to Broken Nose whenever he decided the time was right. Or he might head toward Sundog Cañon, follow it to the river, then light out for Utah. Or he could go directly to Broken Nose and depend on some of his friends giving him an alibi.

He could even hide out on the mesa, and wait until night to escape from Pitchfork range. Even if Shaniko and Dutch John ran into the man, they wouldn't take him because they wouldn't know what he'd done.

A bitter sense of futility took hold of Bill as he hunted. The dry gulcher was putting more distance between them by the minute. He lost all concept of time, goaded by impatience as he was, and, when he finally found the spot where the man's horse had been tied to a cedar, he learned very little except that the killer had ridden in from the east, and he'd headed north when he left.

Bill spent another minute or two finding the place where the man had waited behind another cedar a short distance from where he'd tied his horse. Here he found three .30-30 shells that told him nothing because the .30-30 was the most common rifle on the range. He discovered a reasonably clear boot mark in some soft earth next to the trunk of the cedar. The boot was smaller than average, probably new or nearly so, for the heel was not run over.

Judging from the sign where the bushwhacker had left his horse, he had waited here several hours, but there were no cigarette stubs where the man had waited. Either he had been very careful, or he wasn't a cigarette smoker. If the latter were true, Bill could immediately cut down the number of prospects.

Returning to his horse, Bill rode north, often losing the tracks, and having to swing back and forth until he picked them up again. Once more he was aware he was losing time, but he couldn't do anything else.

Half a mile or so north of the ridge he discovered that the tracks led into an arroyo that angled northwest. After that, he made time because his man followed the wash. At the end of another half mile the dry gulcher climbed the steep west bank, and Bill found himself at the stone cabin where one of the early settlers on the mesa had lived.

Bill had a bad moment, suddenly realizing that the fugitive might guess he'd be pursued, and he'd decide to wait here to cut down anyone who came after him. A man who would dry-gulch Old Mike would not be above doing the same to whoever hunted him.

Bill swung down and ran to the ruins of the cabin, jerking his gun from leather. Nothing left but the walls, the door and windows long gone. No one was inside. Bill leaned against the wall, breathing hard as relief swept through him. He put his gun back into leather, thinking that the man had missed a bet here.

Anyone waiting inside could have cut him down the instant he showed in the doorway.

Bill made a quick study of the dirt floor that was covered with débris. A man and horse had been here for a good many hours. This time Bill found cigarette stubs. So there had been two, this one and the ambusher who had come here to join him. But why? Bill had no answer; it simply failed to make any sense. The Gilberts, maybe. They had more immediate reason to kill Old Mike than anyone else, but why hadn't they been together on the ridge?

When he went outside, he found that the tracks separated. Here on the hard pan he couldn't tell which was which, but by riding around the cabin in a wide circle he discovered that one man had gone east, the other west toward Sundog Cañon. He couldn't make an intelligent guess about which way the bushwhacker had gone, but he sat his saddle, considering this, trying to put himself in the place of the guilty man.

One apparently was going to town, the other was running. Knowing the kind of men who rode for Pitchfork, the dry gulcher could be certain he'd be pursued, so the chances were he'd light a shuck out of the country. With the odds equal, it was this thought that decided Bill. He turned west.

The stone cabin was not more than a quarter of a mile from the rim of the cañon, but now Bill saw the man was definitely on the run. He had ridden hard, making no effort to hide his tracks. He was plainly more interested in putting distance between him and Pitchfork than anything else.

At this point the east wall of the cañon was a sheer precipice, so the fugitive swung downstream, being forced to ride along the rim for two hundred yards or more before he found a side cañon that could be followed to the creek.

A sudden feeling of elation washed through Bill. If his man went upstream, he had him bottled up. He couldn't get out of the cañon between here and Dead Man Falls, and the falls would stop him. If he went downstream, the only place where he could leave the cañon was where Bill had crossed with Vida and Shaniko Red. If he climbed out to the east, he'd be dangerously close to the Pitchfork buildings. If he went west, he'd come out within sight of the line cabin and there was a good chance he'd run into Turk Allen.

He might keep on, following the cañon to the county road that paralleled the river. As Bill continued this line of reasoning, his elation cooled. Once on the road, the man could do any of a number of things. If he sought refuge on one of the ranches south of Skull River, Bill would never find him.

Bill rode down the side cañon, twisting and turning through the narrow passage, dust stirring behind him. At times the rock walls were so close that the sky was a narrow, blue ribbon overhead. He couldn't make time here. He had to let his horse pick his way down the steep slope, but he knew he wasn't losing time, either, for his man wouldn't travel any faster.

When he reached the creek, he saw with keen disappointment that the fugitive had turned downstream; the tracks were easy to read in the mud beside the stream. If the fellow didn't know the country, Bill figured there was an even chance he'd swing up the creek. He might be tricky, reversing himself at the end of the strip of mud and throw his pursuit off by staying in the water, but Bill had a feeling the man was too panicky to be tricky. He continued on down the cañon and presently picked up the tracks again in a sandbar on the opposite side of the stream.

When Bill reached the crossing between the line cabin and headquarters, he found that the fugitive had kept going downstream. Now hope was a low-burning flame in Bill. Once on the river, the avenues of escape were countless. Bill was aware, too, that he could be after the wrong man, a decoy who might purposely be leading him away from the killer. But at least this one knew the other's identity, and Bill would get it out of him.

Half an hour later Bill was on the road. The man had turned west. Wet hoofs had left unmistakable tracks. Presently he lost them, for other horses had been on the road this morning. A mile below the mouth of Sundog Creek, the road to Box H crossed the river and climbed the mesa hill to the south.

Bill got off his horse and made a careful study, but he could not reach a sure decision. At least one rider had gone on down the river. Two others had taken the Box H road. Once more he had to make a blind choice, with only one thing to guide him.

His man was panicky, having made no effort to throw his pursuer off his trail. If he were panicky enough, he'd get out of the country as quickly as he could. So Bill swung again into the saddle, deciding to go west, fully realizing that, if he had guessed right, he might be riding into an ambush just as he might have done at the stone cabin.

Bill put his horse into a ground-eating trot. The road was little more than a trail following the north bank of the river, the hay meadows were behind him. Now the walls narrowed, not as high and sheer as the sides of Sundog Cañon, but steep enough so that there was little chance of the fugitive's leaving the stream. If, of course, Bill had made the right choice and his man was still ahead of him, he would know when he reached Horn's ranch.

The good range country was behind him. Ahead for miles and running deep into Utah was arid country, with only a few scattered ranches, so poor they were incapable of furnishing a living for their owners.

It was outlaw country where a man on the dodge was welcome, where stolen stock could be marketed, where human life was cheap, and where a stranger was viewed with harsh suspicion. Ed Grant never rode past Horn's place without a posse, and then only on rare occasions. The country was too big, too empty, and there were too many places to hide.

The Utah sheriff on the other side of the state line performed in exactly the same manner. To make it worse, bands of Utes often drifted off their reservation in Utah and came across the line to hunt, or simply to kick up a fuss when they felt like it.

The result was that this strip of badlands was actually outside the law. The man Bill was pursuing, unless he was an imported killer who was known out here, might find himself in more trouble than if he'd stood and fought. But he wouldn't think of that, as panicky as he seemed to be. Jake Horn's place was on the edge of this outlaw country. He kept a roadhouse of sorts, putting up anyone who wanted to stay overnight, selling supplies, and, by skilful footwork, contrived to stay out of trouble with both sides. Bill reached Horn's ranch shortly after noon. The house was a long, low building made of cottonwood logs, and was little different from the barn except that it had two glass windows. There were several sheds, a couple of corrals that held half a dozen horses, and a hay meadow below the buildings that he irrigated from the river.

Dismounting, Bill watered his horse at a trough between the house and the barn. He stood there, studying the layout while he made a pretense of being busy with a cigarette. A prickle began working up and down his spine. His man could be in the barn or the house or one of the sheds, drawing a bead on Bill's belly this very instant. A yellow dog ran out of one of the sheds behind the house and began to yap at Bill, scattering half a dozen droopy-combed hens with a deal of cackling and a flurry of dust and feathers. A brown-skinned boy, ten or eleven, followed the dog, yelling at him to shut up. Horn did not appear.

Bill called: "Howdy, bub!"

The boy approached him, a little uncertain, bare feet silent in the dust. He said—"Howdy, mister."—and stood there, blinking, his thumbs hooked in the waistband of his ragged pants.

Bill had never seen the boy before. He knew Jake Horn had a half-breed wife, so the boy would be a quarter Ute, and he showed it with his black hair and dark eyes.

"Your dad home?" Bill asked.

The boy jerked his head at the door. "He's eating dinner."

"Fetch him out, will you?"

The boy hesitated until Bill tossed half a dollar into the dust at his feet. He scooped it up and whirled and ran toward the house. Bill moved so that his horse was between him and the house, half convinced by the way the boy had acted that his man was inside eating dinner with Horn.

Jake didn't appear immediately. As the minutes passed, Bill became certain that his hunch was right. He had seen Horn a few times in Broken Nose, but he wasn't sure the rancher would know him. When Horn did leave the house, he moved slowly, a scowl on his square face. "Howdy," he said as he came up. "You wanted me?"

"Yeah. Thought I might get a meal."

Horn shifted his weight, his red-flecked eyes studying Bill uneasily. Then he turned to stare at the north rim. "Sorry, friend. We just et. You've got to get here afore noon if you're going to eat with us. My wife ain't well." When Bill didn't move, he said: "Might as well mosey on, mister."

"Long ways to the next place," Bill said. "I'm hungry."

"Sorry," Horn said, and started to turn.

"You know who I am?" Bill asked.

"Why, I don't give a small, thin damn," Horn said. "For all I know you might be God."

"I've seen you in Broken Nose," Bill said, "and you've seen me."

"Don't recollect that I ever did," Horn said, and again turned toward the house.

"I'm Bill Varney. Old Mike's my father."

Horn swung back, obviously distressed. He mumbled: "Well, I didn't miss it far, saying you might be God. What do you want me to do, get down on my knees?"

"I want a meal."

"I said no." Horn motioned toward the road. "Hit the dirt, mister. The Varneys cut a wide swath around Broken Nose but they sure as hell don't around here."

"Old Mike was shot this morning and I'm after the killer. You see a stranger go by this morning?"

"No," Horn said. "No stranger. You're wasting your time here."

He turned toward the house again, and this time Bill let him go.

Chapter Twelve

Bill was sure of two things—the man he'd been chasing was within a few yards of him, and he couldn't stay here. He called to Horn: "Looks like I made the wrong turn back there a piece! I'd better light a shuck for town."

He stepped into the saddle and, turning his horse, left Horn's yard and started back the way he'd come. He held himself under rigid discipline, refusing to give way to his impulse to look back. As soon as he was out of sight around a bend in the road, he put his horse across the river, which was swift and shallow at this point, then turned downstream toward Horn's ranch.

He rode as far as he dared, remaining close to the willows along the south bank of the stream. When he wasn't sure that the leafy screen of willows still hid him from Horn's buildings, he dismounted, tied his horse, and, keeping low, ran forward until he had a good view of Horn's yard. He dropped down on his belly and lay motionlessly. A minute or so later Horn left the house with a tray of food in one hand and a coffee pot in the other, and strode to the barn.

Now Bill had the answer he wanted. The man he was after was in the barn, not the house. This was as good a time as any to make his move. For a minute or two both Horn and the dry gulcher would have their attention diverted. Perhaps they wouldn't be watching anyhow, thinking that Bill was a mile away by this time.

He was about fifty yards from the nearest shed, with no cover between him and the shed, an open field that he crossed on the dead run. He expected a bullet, and if the man shot as straight as he had at Old Mike that morning, he was a dead man. But he reached the shed with nothing happening. He leaned against the wall, panting hard, and then went on to the house. Horn was still in the barn.

Bill reached the back door, opened it, and went in without knocking. A woman was bending over the stove, her back to him. She heard the door and whirled. It was Horn's wife, Bill thought, not as dark of skin as he expected, but with the heavy features of the Utes. Mrs. Horn wasn't tall, but she was heavy and strong, and Bill knew he had trouble the minute she saw him. She didn't scream as most women would have done. She simply picked up a butcher knife from the top of the warming oven and started toward him.

"No!" he yelled at her. "I'm not here to hurt you! Put that knife down!"

She didn't obey. She didn't even hesitate or say a word. Her swarthy face did not show fear or hate or any strong emotion. She walked toward him with the long, shiny-bladed knife held in front of her as if she meant to cut his heart out. She'd do it, too, he thought, if he stood there and let her do it.

When she was five feet away, he jumped sideways. She moved with him, still facing him, and lunged forward, striking at him with the knife, a vicious stab that would have disemboweled him if it had found its mark. Again he moved sideways, and for a second he had her off balance. He gripped her wrist and twisted it.

"Drop the knife!" he shouted. "Damn it, drop the knife! I'm not trying to hurt you or your husband!"

"You'll kill my boy," she said.

She struggled with him, still holding the knife, then she struck him on the cheek with her left hand, a hard blow that rocked his head. He swore at her, jamming her back against the table and knocking it over, dishes clattering to the floor.

She was as heavy as he was and stronger than a good many men he'd tangled with. What she'd said about her boy made no sense to him. If Horn came back while he was fighting the woman, he'd get shot before he could explain why he was here.

He shoved her back against the wall, still holding her wrist and twisting it, a shoulder hard against her chest. He held her that way so she was unable to move her body. She kicked him, her moccasin-clad foot doing no damage. She dipped her head forward, trying to bite him. He stepped back, releasing the pressure as he yanked her by the wrist, a hard jerk that sent her whirling like a top. She dropped the knife and he kicked it across the room.

"Behave, damn it!" he shouted. "I don't want to hurt you or your husband or your boy."

He moved back, his gun in his hand. She stood motionlessly, glaring at him and saying nothing. They were that way when Jake Horn came in, carrying the tray and coffee pot. He stopped, blinking, confused by what he saw.

"Horn, don't make me any trouble," Bill said. "I'm not fighting you. When I came in, your wife jumped me with a butcher knife."

"All right, Lucy," Horn said heavily. "Let him alone. We'll have to tell him what happened."

"No," she said.

Horn was silent while he put the tray and coffee pot on the floor and set the table back on its legs. Then he placed the tray and coffee pot on the table, and motioned for his wife to pick up the dishes.

"Fix a meal for him, Lucy," Horn said. "We've got to tell him. Put your gun up, Varney."

"Have you got it through your wife's head I don't mean her

any harm?" Bill asked.

"It ain't her she's worried about," Horn said. "It's our oldest boy Chris." He looked at his wife who hadn't moved. "Lucy, damn it, you want me to take an axe handle to you?"

She set to work then, picking up the mess from the floor. Bill slid his gun back into his holster, warily eyeing her, but now she ignored him.

Horn shoved a chair at Bill. "Sit down, Varney." He got his pipe out and filled it, his face filled with misery. "Your man's out there in the barn, but you can't go after him. I'll kill you if you try it. Or Lucy will."

"What the hell's going on?" Bill demanded. "I don't see what I've got to do with your boy. . . ."

"He's got Chris in the barn with him," Horn said. "That's why I acted the way I done when you was out front. He rode in a little while afore you did. Didn't say a word. Just put his horse in the barn and waited, watching the road. Chris and Skip, that's the little feller, went over to him, curious like. I was in the house washing up for dinner and didn't see what was going on. Well, this bastard grabbed Chris soon as he got close and told Skip to fetch me."

Horn tamped the tobacco into the bowl of his pipe, then slipped the sack back into his shirt pocket. "Varney, you know how it is out here. Half the bad ones in the country drift up and down the outlaw trail, a lot of 'em stopping here for a meal or to buy supplies. I pretend I don't know who they are, but I do business with 'em and they don't bother me. Or my family, neither. But that coyote out there in the barn tops 'em all."

Horn lit his pipe, his hand trembling. Then he shook the match out and threw it on the floor. "When I got there, he had Chris in front of him, the gun pointed at his head. He told me to fetch some grub. He was gonna stay there till dark. Somebody like you might be along after him, but I'd better get rid of you or he'd shoot Chris." Horn spread his hands. "You see how it was, and why Lucy jumped you like she done. She figured you'd go tearing out there after this booger and he'd kill Chris, which he would if you acted the fool."

"I won't," Bill said. He looked at Horn's wife. "You understand, Lucy? We'll figure something out, but not till we've got your boy back."

She nodded and kept on working. Horn jerked his head at Bill and walked into the front room, Bill following. Horn went to the window. "Stand to one side so he can't see you. I don't think he'll hurt Chris if we don't push him. But he's sure jumpy. Never saw a scareder man. He ain't no outlaw like I'm used to dealing with. They'll shoot a man when they hold up a bank or a train if they have to, but they're decent, and I never saw one act scared. But this bastard! He was trembling and his mouth was quivering and slobber was pouring down his chin. He couldn't even talk good."

"Who is he?"

"Dunno," Horn said. "He's young. Big. Got a round head like a billiard ball. His face is marked up some, like he'd been in a scrap recent like."

"Lud Gilbert," Bill said. "Old Charlie Gilbert's boy."

"I should've knowed," Horn said. "I've stopped a couple of times at the Hell Hole for a drink afore I went on into town. I never seen this one, but I had seen Charlie, and the boy looks like him, now that you mention it."

So it had been Lud Gilbert, panicky, heading out of the country on the run, leaving his father and Annie Bain somewhere behind him with the calves and a pile of ashes that had been the Hell Hole. Maybe Old Mike was dead by now, but it wasn't over. Taking Lud back wouldn't finish it, either. To Charlie Gilbert and Sid Kehoe and the rest of the south mesa ranchers, Pitchfork was the enemy, and they wouldn't rest until it was destroyed.

"What are you going to do?" Horn asked.

"I don't know," Bill said. "How is your boy?"

"He's scared. Reckon any of us would be, but he's eighteen. He's a man grown and in a pinch he'll act like one."

It was hot there in the log house, hot and stifling with the front door closed. A blow fly made an irritating buzz against a window. Bill swatted at it with his hand, and missed. It flew away and returned a moment later to pick up his buzzing where he had left off.

Bill wiped his face with his bandanna, knowing he had to get back to town and see the sheriff and find out how Old Mike was. He had to see Marian, had to keep her from marrying Phil Nider. He had to settle with Turk Allen.

Now, for the first time in his life, he saw his and Vida's future. Old Mike might die, or he might linger along for months. Either way, he wouldn't be running Pitchfork for a while. Neither would Turk Allen, if Bill had anything to do with it.

So it would be up to him. Somehow he had to change the picture that people of Broken Nose and the ranchers south of the river had of Pitchfork. He had to make promises to them, assure them, convince them, that from here on out it was going to be different, that Pitchfork would be content with the grass it had, willing to live and let live. It boiled down to one basic thing that must be done, and he had to do it by himself, or with Vida's help. What Old Mike had done for twenty years had to be undone as nearly as it could.

You couldn't give a man's life back. You couldn't even give grass back to people who had sold out and left the country, or been driven out. It was the future that had to be changed so it wouldn't follow the pattern of the past, but the first problem was to see that Pitchfork survived.

"Well?" Horn asked.

The single word prodded Bill back into the present. He wiped his face again and shook his head. "I don't know, Horn," he said. "I sure don't."

Lucy called for him to come to the kitchen. He did, leaving Horn by the window. He ate mechanically, hardly tasting the food, his mind on Lud Gilbert out in the barn, but he still didn't know what to do.

CHAPTER THIRTEEN

When Bill finished eating and returned to the window, he found Jake Horn standing there as if he hadn't moved. Bill said: "When you took the grub to Lud, where was he sitting and where was your boy?"

"Gilbert had put his horse in a stall," Horn said. "He wasn't sitting. He was leaning against the back wall. Chris was sitting on the ground about twenty feet away. Gilbert had his gun on him. He had me put the grub on the floor, then he made Chris fetch it to him and go back and sit where he had been. He told me he'd be moving around, so I'd better not figure on sneaking to the back of the barn and shooting through the wall. There's some knotholes on this side, and he said he'd be looking through them once in a while. He said he'd shoot Chris the first time I made what looked like a wrong move. I believe he would, Varney."

Bill nodded agreement, convinced that Horn was right, but Gilbert was tired and scared, and probably sleepy. Bill asked: "How big's your boy?"

"Taller'n me, but he ain't got much beef on him. Why?"

"Suppose Gilbert went to sleep? Or we did something that distracted him? Would Chris jump him?"

"No, Gilbert's too big for him. Besides, I told him to do what Gilbert ordered."

"Is there any way you could give Chris a hunch if you went out there with a pot of coffee?"

"Don't think so. What kind of a notion have you got?"

"We've got to kick this loose some way," Bill said. "I've been looking at that damned barn ever since I got here, and I can't figure any way to get to it without being seen. Even if I waded along the river and got around to the other side, I wouldn't be any better off."

"You sure wouldn't." Horn whirled to face him, impelled by sudden violence. "You'd just get Chris plugged. Why don't you go back? You can't do no good here."

"You're wrong," Bill said. "We've just got to figure out what's the best way of getting at it. If I did leave, you don't know he wouldn't wipe all of you out before he rode off."

"Hell, he wouldn't do that."

"You can't tell, the way he's feeling." Bill shook his head. "Chances are he's sitting out there, thinking he'd be crazy to go off and leave four witnesses alive who have seen him and know he's been here. He'll figure that sooner or later I'll be back when I find out he didn't go south back to town."

Horn swore. "You could be right, Varney." He glared at Bill. "Maybe you know how to root him out of his hole?"

"I do," Bill said, "But I'm not sure it'll work. We've got to do something, so I think it's worth a try. Have your wife put some coffee on. Tell her to fill a sack with some grub."

Horn showed his doubt, but he went into the kitchen, talked briefly to his wife, and returned. "All right, how do we play it?"

"We don't know whether he's watching or not," Bill said, "but we've got to go on the basis that he is. If I walked out there, I'd start the ball and we don't want that. But you could go, taking the coffee and the grub to him. Tell him it's going to rain. Maybe it will. There's some clouds boiling up yonder. He might believe it. Tell him he'd be smart to put all the distance he can between him and here. When it rains, it'll wash his tracks out. Then nobody can trail him."

"What then?"

"He'll bring his horse to the trough and water him. That'll put him about halfway between here and the barn. Just as he's getting into the saddle, I'll run out and get my gun on him. I ought to cover ten, maybe twenty feet before he sees me on account of he'll be talking to you. He'll throw up his hands or he'll shoot, and, if he does, I'll be close enough to get him. If he quits, I'll take him to town."

Horn shook his head. "You take him to town, Varney, and what'll happen? His dad will come after me. Or he'll get loose and show up here. I've never sold any of the boys out who stop here. I ain't starting now."

"Lud Gilbert isn't one of the boys," Bill said. "It's a pretty long shot that he'd get out of jail. Charlie won't show up. He's got too much to think about."

Horn's face turned stubborn. "I won't do it."

"You afraid to walk from here to the barn?"

"Hell, no. I just figure the safest way to play it is to do what he said. He'll leave, come dark, and we'll never see him again."

"If you're still alive, which I doubt you will be." Bill rolled and lit a smoke, tension making his fingers awkward. "Horn, maybe you don't know it, but Ed Grant's had his eye on you for quite a spell. I reckon all I can do is to go back to Broken Nose and tell him."

Bill turned and reached the kitchen door before Horn said: "All right, all right, but if this don't work, Varney, I'll skin you and hang your hide on my front door to dry."

"Let's take care of Gilbert first," Bill said, and returned to the window. "I can't promise it'll work. All we can do is to play it the way that seems to us to give the best odds."

Horn said nothing to that. He went back to the kitchen and waited until the coffee was ready. Sweat kept running down Bill's face from his forehead. The house was oven hot, and the fire in the kitchen range added to it. Bill wiped his face; his shirt was clinging to the small of his back. His heart was pounding in his chest with great sledge-hammer blows. He was afraid, not for himself as much as for Jake Horn and his boy Chris.

There was no way to tell how a thing like this would work. Lud Gilbert, unless Bill's action was timed perfectly, might cut down both the Horns before Bill got him. He would never forgive himself if it went wrong. On the other hand, it might go wrong if he rode back home and did nothing.

Presently Horn came out of the kitchen carrying a flour sack of food in one hand and a steaming pot of coffee in the other. As he crossed the room, Bill said: "When I open the ball, you get the boy out of the way. And leave the door open as you go out."

Horn remained silent. He was plainly nervous, and he had a right to be, Bill thought. Lud Gilbert might consider bringing the coffee to him a wrong move and start shooting.

Horn crossed the yard, moving slowly and deliberately. When he reached the horse trough, he called: "Hey, I've got some coffee for you!" He went on. When he was within ten feet of the barn door, it opened and he entered. The door swung shut behind him without Bill getting a glimpse of Lud.

Bill drew his gun, checked it, and slid it back into leather. He rubbed his moist hands up and down on his pants legs. He felt sweat run down his body and on down his legs. The open door didn't help. It was as hot outside, or hotter, than it was inside the log house. The barn would be hot, too. It might be a factor that would help Gilbert decide to leave. Bill had some idea of the tension the man was under, wanting to run and still held by a notion that he shouldn't be seen.

Bill heard the sullen mutter of distant thunder. He hoped Gilbert heard it, too. That might be another factor that would make him decide to leave now. The black clouds were moving this way, and lightning was playing along the horizon. But the approaching storm had not changed the heat except to make it sticky.

He had little notion of time. He was waiting, the kind of dragging waiting that tightened a man's nerves and made him feel that each plodding minute that passed so slowly would be an hour if measured by a clock.

Then the door opened and Lud Gilbert came out of the barn, leading his horse. Bill drew his gun and held it at his side, tense, watchful. The boy didn't appear, but Jake Horn did, walking beside Gilbert who came on to the horse trough.

They stood talking, looking westward at the clouds, Horn motioning as if giving directions. Gilbert tightened his cinch, looked at the sack of grub tied behind the saddle, then said something to Horn, and stepped up. Bill chose that exact instant to charge through the door and go on the dead run toward Gilbert.

Bill took three or four long strides before Gilbert had his attention diverted from Horn, either by the blur of movement or the pound of Bill's boots. Gilbert turned his head, saw him, and let out a bellow of rage. He jerked his gun as Bill yelled: "Hoist 'em, Lud! Hook the moon."

Instead, Lud tried to bring his gun into line. Bill threw a shot, creasing the horse along the rump and causing him to pitch so that Lud's shot went wild.

Horn sprinted toward the barn door. Lud dug in his spurs and yanked at the reins with his left hand, clubbing his gun down for another shot. The bullet kicked up dust at Bill's feet. Bill fired again and missed. Lud had his horse under control then, and drove straight at Bill, intending to ride him down.

Bill's third shot caught him in the middle and sent him pinwheeling out of the saddle to fall hard, spread-eagled and motionless. The horse bucked across the yard. Bill ran forward, hammer pronged back. Gilbert had lost his gun. He rolled over, grabbed for it, and raised himself to his hands and knees. He had the gun in his hand and was tilting it into line when Bill reached him and kicked it halfway to the horse trough.

Standing directly over Gilbert, Bill pointed his gun at the man's head. "You're going to town, Lud. Try anything else and you're a dead pigeon."

Gilbert was flat on his back now, the hot sunlight on his dust-smeared face. He put a hand over the bullet hole in his middle. Blood seeped around his fingers and made a spreading stain on his shirt just above the belt buckle.

"I'm a dead pigeon anyway." He closed his eyes, left hand knotted at his side, right trying to stop the flow of blood. "No sense of me running. I just got boogered. I didn't shoot Old Mike."

Bill dropped to his knees. "Who did?"

The eyes came open for a moment, wild and frantic. "You killed me, Varney, but you got the wrong man."

Bill reached out to shake him. "Who did it?" He dropped his hand to his side. No use. The man was dead.

Bill rose and holstered his gun. There was a sack of Bull Durham in Gilbert's shirt pocket. He had big feet; the heels of both boots were run over on the sides. Now, staring at the dead man, Bill remembered the cigarette stubs inside the old stone cabin, but there had been none under the cedar tree where the dry gulcher had waited for Old Mike to appear. A small boot with the sharp imprint of a heel that wasn't run over.

Lud Gilbert had waited in the stone cabin, but he wasn't the man under the cedar tree who had pulled the trigger on Old Mike Varney. Bill knew it with as much certainty as if he had seen with his own eyes what had happened. But why had Lud waited in the stone cabin? And why had he run, so panicky that he had thought of nothing except headlong escape?

Horn came up, walking slowly in the tired way of a man who has been squeezed dry of all feeling. He said wearily: "He took it, line, hook, and sinker."

"How's the boy?"

"All right, or will be when he gets over the shakes." Horn looked at Bill, running a tongue over cracked lips. "You figured it right. Gilbert kept telling Chris you'd gone back, and, if we was all dead, nobody'd ever know he stopped here."

"Well, you're alive. Get his horse and load him on it. I'm taking him to town."

As Bill turned away to go after his horse, Horn asked: "You ain't gonna say anything to Grant about me? I mean, what I told you about the ridge runners going through here?"

"Hell, no," Bill said. "Nothing I could tell him he doesn't already know."

Half an hour later he was on his way back up the river, past the mouth of Sundog Creek, past the charred remains of what had been the Hell Hole with its blackened, twisted bedsteads, and on toward Broken Nose. The night settled around him as clouds moved on across the sky toward the Flat Tops, and the thunder was louder now and closer.

He was tired, more tired than he had ever been in his life, and he felt worse when he remembered that his long chase had accomplished exactly nothing. He still did not know the identity of the man who had shot Old Mike Varney.

CHAPTER FOURTEEN

As long as he lived, Phil Nider would never forget that moment of sheer ecstasy when he drew a bead on Old Mike Varney and squeezed the trigger and saw him go down. It seemed to him that Clara was there beside him. He thought he heard her say: "Why didn't you do that a long time ago, Phil?"

He fired two more times, not really caring whether he scored again or not. He was sure that Old Mike was either dead or dying. He left three empty shells on the ground, knowing that they wouldn't point to him any more than to half the other men on this range who hated Old Mike, and ran to his horse.

He jammed his Winchester into the boot, suddenly realizing he should have taken this opportunity to shoot Bill, too. With him out of the way, he'd have no trouble persuading Marian to marry him, and two killings didn't represent any more danger than one. But it was too late now. He had fastened his hatred on Old Mike so fiercely that he'd had no room in his mind for anything else. That was a mistake, of course.

Now that he was into this, he couldn't afford sentiment of any kind. He had to think coldly and clearly. There was no turning back, no side-stepping. The fire was burning. All he had to do was to keep throwing on fuel.

When he reached the stone cabin, he called: "Lud!" Carefully young Gilbert looked out of the window, the glass long gone, a gaping eye between the door and the corner. "Old Mike's dead," Nider said. "Get on your horse and head west. As soon as you get to Sundog Cañon, drop downstream till you find a side cañon. Ride to the creek, follow it to the river, and then get out of the country. You can get in touch with your dad after this cools off."

Lud didn't move. He just blinked as if he couldn't quite grasp what Nider was saying. Finally he muttered: "Hell, I didn't plug the old man."

"You think anybody'll believe you after what happened to your dad and Whitey Matts and the Hell Hole?" Nider asked. "If Bill or Shaniko Red find you on Pitchfork range, they'll hang you so high you won't even see the ground."

Nider whirled his horse away from the stone cabin and rode east. He glanced back once and saw that Lud Gilbert was in the saddle and going in the other direction. He laughed silently and pulled his horse down to a slower pace. If he ran into any of the Pitchfork cowhands, he didn't want to seem in a hurry. That was the advantage of appearing to be a man just casually riding.

No one, he was certain, would think that soft-spoken, precise Phil Nider was capable of killing a man, but all this time he had been killing Old Mike Varney in his heart. Now it was actually done, and again he lived in memory that sweet, sweet moment when Old Mike had stumbled and gone down with Nider's .30-30 slug in his guts.

He was three miles north of Broken Nose when he reached the county road that ran north to the Yampa Valley. He turned toward town and traveled fifty yards or more before it struck him that he'd better have an alibi for the morning just as a plain, common-sense precaution.

The Combs horse ranch was another five miles to the north, a small island surrounded by Pitchfork grass. The only reason it survived was because Benjy Combs raised and trained horses for Old Mike. Combs didn't have a cow on his place, so Old Mike tolerated him as long as he had his pick of Combs's horses. It would not be a perfect alibi, but it would do. It was not unusual for him to take an early morning ride, and Mrs. O'Toole wouldn't, and actually couldn't swear that he had not slept in his room the last half of the night.

He spent most of the day with Benjy Combs, amiably wrangling over the price of a gentle sorrel mare. He wanted her for Marian, he told Combs, a present he'd promised the girl weeks ago. He just hadn't got around to coming up here before.

By the time they agreed on the price, it was time to head for town. He got back in time for supper. As he stripped gear from his horse, he realized his rifle presented a problem. It had to be cleaned, but he didn't want Mrs. O'Toole to know he had taken it with him, so he hid it under the hay in the mow and went in through the back door.

After supper he shaved and changed his clothes, then walked through the thinning dusk light to the Tracey house. Marian was busy with her mother in the old lady's bedroom, so Nider had to wait in the kitchen, impatience gnawing at him.

As the minutes passed, his temper roughened and he thought what a hell of a situation he'd have if he married Marian while her mother was still alive. He'd have less than half a wife, with the old lady demanding this and that. Why, Marian probably couldn't even leave town for a honeymoon.

If Mrs. Tracey had her operation and died . . . or, if she just died, as any old woman should who had complained as long as she had, the future would be solved, providing, of course, that Bill Varney was out of the way, or if Marian had already promised to marry Nider.

When Marian finally came into the kitchen and lit a lamp, she looked more tired than Nider had ever seen her. She built up the fire and put the coffee pot on the front of the stove, then she turned to Nider. She said: "I'm awfully sorry I had to make you wait like this, but it's always a ceremony getting Ma to bed.

The pillows have to be just right and her slippers have to be at the edge of the bed and her glasses on the night stand. I have to rub her back and. . . ." She stopped, wiping a hand across her face. "Forgive me, Phil. I didn't intend to bother you with my troubles."

He rose and, walking to her, took her hands. He said gently: "I want to share your troubles, Marian. I've told you that many times, but you never seem to believe me."

There were tears in her eyes when she looked at him. "I do believe you, Phil. It's just that you have your own life, a very pleasant one with a good business and a housekeeper and no real problems."

"I have my problems, Marian," he said gravely. "You're my biggest one. I keep asking you to marry me and you keep putting me off. I love you and I'm going to keep on asking you. I need you and I think you need me."

She turned from him and, walking into the pantry, returned with a chocolate cake. "I baked this for you. I thought you'd call. Or maybe I just hoped you would." She brought cream and sugar, plates and forks and spoons. "You will eat a piece, won't you?"

"Of course I will." He cleared his throat, then added: "Marian, I spent the day with Benjy Combs. I bought a present for you. A wedding present, I hope. Can you guess what it is?"

A quick smile softened her lips, her blue eyes brightened, and suddenly the tired lines that marred her face were gone. "A saddle horse is the only thing you could buy from Benjy Combs."

"That's right. You remember that little sorrel mare of his. Benjy brought her into town last spring and you saw her and admired her. She's gentle. Missus Combs has ridden her several times."

"You're good, Phil, you're wonderfully good, but I think this is a bribe. If I don't marry you, I don't get the mare. Is that it?"

He laughed. "I'm not that mercenary, but, if you're open to bribery, I'm open to making an offer." He walked to where she stood at the table. He said earnestly: "I'm going to propose again, Marian. You need help with your mother. You need money for that operation. If you were my wife and living in my house, Missus O'Toole could help you. I admit I'm selfish. I want you so much I'll do anything and everything I can that you need or want done."

"You're not selfish, Phil," she flared. "Don't say you are." She paused, then turned and cut the cake. With her back to him, she said: "I won't lie to you, Phil. I don't love you. Not the way I think I should love my husband, but I do like you. I'll try to be a good wife, and maybe in time. . . ."

"Marian." He put his hands on her shoulders and made her turn to face him. "Then you will marry me?"

"Yes, I'll marry you, Phil, if you understand. . . ."

"I understand perfectly." He kissed her, and for the first time he sensed a stir of emotion in her, a giving of herself to him in a way he never had felt before, and suddenly he was young again, as young as when he had fallen in love with Clara Varney almost twenty years ago.

When he let her go, she smiled at him and motioned for him to draw his chair up to the table. "I think the coffee's ready, Phil. Let's celebrate with a piece of cake."

"I wish we had champagne to celebrate with," he said. "I'll get word to Benjy to fetch that mare to town, and I'll send to Denver for a ring. I'll get you the biggest diamond you ever saw."

"No, Phil," she said. "Just a little one. I'm not a clothes horse. I can dress up other people, but I can't do much for myself. A big diamond would look out of place on my finger."

"No, it wouldn't. You've been working so hard, doing for

your mother and all, that you haven't had time to think about yourself. Now you set the date and we'll go to Denver for our honeymoon and. . . ."

"Phil, you know how Ma is. I couldn't leave, with her feeling the way she does."

"All right," he said quickly. "We'll put the honeymoon off until you can go."

They ate in silence, the good feeling gone. It seemed to Nider that Mrs. Tracey had walked into the room and was standing between them. He finished his coffee and shook his head at Marian when she started to get up.

"No more, thanks." He cleared his throat. "I'll go see Doc Ripple about that operation." He hesitated, then said: "It's too bad she can't just slip off some night, suffering the way she does. She can't get much pleasure out of living."

Marian was silent and he was afraid he had offended her. It had been a trial balloon and he wished he hadn't launched it. He started to apologize, but before he got the first word out, Marian said: "If I said that, and then she did slip off, I'd feel guilty the rest of my life. She might, too. Her heart gives her lots of trouble."

He hadn't offended her. She wished the old bitch was gone just as much as he did. A hell of a note when Mrs. Tracey kept on living and nobody wanted her to. He said: "You shouldn't ever feel guilty, Marian. You've been more faithful than anyone else I know."

He heard Mrs. Tracey's querulous voice calling Marian. He said: "I've got to go. I'll see you tomorrow." He kissed her, then he asked: "You will marry me, no matter what?"

"No matter what," she said. "And just a little diamond, Phil. You promise?"

"I promise," he said, and went out through the back door. He walked slowly toward the business block, thinking that Mrs.

Tracey would start yelling for Marian on their wedding night just about the time they got into bed. She'd lived too long already. Sometimes the Lord was dilatory about things like that, and, when He was, you had to give Him a hand.

Nider found Dr. Ripple still in his drugstore. He said: "Doc, Marian and I are getting married. Soon, I hope."

The doctor laughed and shook Nider's hand. He stroked his beard as he said expansively: "I guess you'll need a little medical advice, Phil. Now when a young woman marries an old buck like you. . . ."

"I'm not old," Nider cut in hotly, "and I don't need any medical advice about me. It's about Marian's mother. I understand she needs an operation."

Ripple laughed again. "Just like you need another store in town to run you out of business. What that old lady ought to have is a good kick in the seat in the direction of the kitchen. If I was Marian, I'd give it to her."

"She's got a bad heart. . . ."

"Hogwash." Ripple snorted. "I drop in and see her every day or two because she's got to tell somebody about her aches and pains, and I can spell Marian off a little. Missus Tracey's an interesting case to me because I've never had one like her before. She's convinced herself and everybody else that she's sick. I've read of cases like that, but I never thought I'd run into one as flagrant as hers. I'm going to write it up for some medical journal when I get around to it."

"But she told me she needed an operation. . . ."

"Sure," Ripple said, "but you won't catch me cutting into her. I agree with everything she says and sympathize with her. Next week it'll be something else. Sorry, Phil, but you're going to be stuck with a mother-in-law until you're ninety-two. And to think that old woman is five years younger than me and as strong as a horse. Say, did you hear about Old Mike?"

"No," Nider said casually. "I've been out of town all day. At Benjy Combs's ranch. I bought a mare for Marian. What about Old Mike?"

"Got plugged this morning. Somebody done it from the top of that ridge north of the house."

"Who was it?"

The doctor shrugged. "Nobody knows for sure. Ed Grant figures it's Lud Gilbert. Charlie's in town but Lud isn't. Nobody's seen him since they got burned out."

"Well, Lud had reason to do it, I guess," Nider said. "How's Charlie feeling?"

"Ornery. Of course, his arm hurts like hell, but he could get out and ride tonight if he wanted to. Just sits in his hotel room, drinking Chauncey Morts's whiskey and cussing the Varneys. If he hangs around, he'll be able to take another whack at Old Mike himself."

"I thought you said Old Mike was dead."

"Hell, no! Got a slug through him but it didn't hit anything vital. It would take a lot to kill that old bastard."

Nider turned, calling—"Good night, Doc!"—and walked out, an actual physical sickness crawling through him. If he stayed there, Ripple would see that something was wrong with him. For once he knew he could not show the town the serene, detached face that his neighbors had looked upon for so long.

Once in the street, he sat down on a bench, not wanting to go home. For a little while he had felt as if the world were his, perfect, without blemish, the kind of world he had mentally pictured in his mind when Clara was alive. Well, he'd take care of Old Mike yet, and next time he'd shoot him through the head. Old Mike was tough, but he wasn't tough enough to live with a bullet in his brain. As far as Mrs. Tracey went, he'd figure out how to take care of her.

The light in the drugstore winked out. The street was almost dark except for the lights in the Stockade and the hotel lobby. He was still sitting there when he heard someone riding into town. He rose and pressed back into the shadows. When the horseman passed the Stockade, he saw it was Bill Varney, his stubble-covered, dusty face looking more formidable than he had ever seen it before. A lot of Old Mike there. Funny, Nider thought. He had never noticed it before. Not this much, anyhow.

Bill reined up in front of the drugstore. Nider stepped to the edge of the boardwalk, saying: " 'Evening, Bill. You're riding late."

"Yeah, too late," Bill said as he dismounted.

"Who have you got there?"

"Lud Gilbert. I shot him this afternoon."

"Lud Gilbert," Nider repeated. "Well, son, you're in for trouble, what with you shooting Ace Kehoe and now this. A lot of folks have hated your dad for years and they'll be taking it out on you. And Vida. They'll wipe Pitchfork off the face of the map if you let them."

"You'd like that, I guess."

"You've got no call to say that," Nider said indignantly. "It's just that I hear talk, being in the store like I am."

"Then after this you give them some talk back," Bill said. "Let them know Pitchfork's going to be here a long time."

He strode past Nider and pounded on the front door of the drugstore. Nider moved away, then stopped and looked back. As tired as Bill was, he might stay in town. And if he did. . . .

Suddenly it struck Nider that he'd lived without violence for twenty years, a bank robber and a killer who had turned to the respected and quiet life of a cow-town merchant. Now that life was behind him, too. He had thought he'd killed a man today. He was planning on killing an old woman. A third killing would make no difference.

Thinking of Bill Varney's hard, angular face, he realized he had completely underestimated him. Young Varney had to go. He was too dangerous to be permitted to live. Nider remembered how it had been years ago. Murder was a treadmill. Once you started it, you couldn't stop it, and you couldn't get off.

CHAPTER FIFTEEN

When Dr. Ripple unlocked the front door of his drugstore, Bill said: "I've got something for you." He went back to Lud Gilbert's horse, untied the body, and carried it through the store to the back room.

Ripple followed, muttering: "Don't know why I ever studied medicine. Seems like I'm an undertaker a hell of a lot more'n I'm a doctor."

"Seen Old Mike today?" Bill asked.

"Spent most of the day with the old bull-head."

"How is he?"

"Alive. And kicking."

"Is he going to make it?"

Ripple shrugged. "I'm no prophet, but, unless something happens, he'll pull through fine. He didn't bleed much. The slug made a nice, clean hole. Of course, he suffered some shock, but the main problem is to keep him in bed. He should stay there for a long time." He jabbed Bill's chest with a forefinger. "And you oughta be running the outfit, son."

"I aim to," Bill said.

Ripple motioned to the dead man. "Is he the one who did it?"

"I thought so, but just before he died, he said he wasn't."

The doctor pulled at his beard, scowling. "Well, sir, I've never known a dying man to lie. I'd say you'd better keep on looking."

"I aim to do that, too," Bill said, and left the drugstore.

He took Lud's horse to the livery stable, then got Ed Grant out of bed and told him what had happened. The sheriff leaned back in his chair and ran a hand through his tousled hair. He said in a cranky voice: "You've been right busy lately, Bill."

"You fixing to hold me for this killing?" Bill demanded. "I was doing your job, or what you would have done if you'd been there. I didn't have time to come after you."

Grant nodded. "Sure, you done right. I ain't holding you. It would have been a hell of a thing if he'd wiped Horn and his family out. He was probably just bluffing, but, when a man's on the run that way, you don't know what he would have done." He scratched his nose, then got up and began walking around the room in his stocking feet. "Why do you suppose he took off that way if he didn't shoot Old Mike?"

"I don't know," Bill said. "I don't even know what he was doing on Pitchfork range."

"I sure don't like the way things are shaping up," Grant said, returning to his chair and sitting down. "Charlie Gilbert's been in his hotel room all day. First thing this morning he sent Annie Bain for me. When I got there, he wanted to know what I was going to do about the bunch that burned him out. I said I'd ride out there and see if I could find any evidence. He gave me a cussing and said to forget it. He'd take care of it himself."

Grant got up and started walking around the room again. "I've seen this coming for a long time, Bill. All of us here in town have. Frank Burnham. Doc Ripple. And me. We've talked about it. You can't treat people like Old Mike's done without having it come back on you. Now it's here. Ace Kehoe dead. Lud Gilbert dead. Whitey Matts with a cracked noggin, home in bed."

"It's all me, Ed," Bill said.

"No, it ain't," the sheriff snapped. "Every damned thing that's happened goes back to Old Mike. It's just taken it a long time to come to a head. Now word's gone out all over the south mesa. Sid Kehoe's been to see Charlie. Pete Matts, too. Some of the rest. They don't talk to me. They look at me like they don't even see me. It's going to blow, Bill, and I'm damned if I know how to stop it."

"When?"

Grant shrugged. "Not tonight. Takes a little time and a little planning. More of 'em will be in town tomorrow, so it might be tomorrow night. Maybe the next night."

Bill rose. "Ed, there's only one way to stop it. You've got to make that bunch believe we don't want their grass. Sid Kehoe and Charlie Gilbert will be after me just to get square, but the rest of 'em won't trail along unless they think they're fighting for their range."

"How do you figure I can make 'em believe anything like that?" Grant demanded. "You know as well as I do that Old Mike will never change. Come fall, he'll move across the river. He's told me so himself."

"No," Bill said. "I'm going to run Pitchfork, and I'm not moving across the river."

"Talk sense," Grant said irritably. "Sure Old Mike's laid up, but what he can't do, Turk Allen can. I've got a hunch Turk is more to blame than Old Mike is."

"I'm going to fire Turk," Bill said. "I don't know how long I can stay in the saddle, but it'll be as long as Dad's in bed."

He left the house. Grant stared after him as if he believed Bill had gone loco. And maybe he had, Bill thought as he swung into the saddle. He could take care of Turk, and with a little time he could handle Vida. If Old Mike died, there would be peace on this range, but if he lived and regained his strength, Bill could do nothing. There'd be another Turk Allen, and everything would go back to where it had been before Old Mike was wounded. Ed Grant was right in saying Old Mike would never change.

Bill had intended to ride back to Pitchfork tonight, but now he changed his mind. What he had to do at Pitchfork could be done better in the morning. Besides, he wanted to see Marian, and it was too late to call tonight. So he turned toward Main Street.

When he reached the end of the block, he glanced back. He caught a furtive movement on the walk. Someone was following him.

He dug in his spurs, whirling his horse around and grabbing his Colt. He expected to hear a gun, maybe have a bullet knock him out of the saddle, but nothing happened. Whoever had been there had slipped back into the impenetrable shadows between Ed Grant's house and his neighbor's. It would be suicide to follow.

He turned his horse again and this time rode on to the stable, then went to the hotel and got a room. He locked the door, threw his hat on the bureau, dropped his gun belt at the head of his bed, and pulled off his boots. He lay down, leaving his clothes on. He was tired, so tired he felt he couldn't move. Hungry, too, for he'd had nothing to eat since noon.

For a long time he lay awake, ears strained for any sound that was not a normal night racket. There was little noise of any kind. Unless a bunch of cowhands were in town, blowing off steam, Broken Nose rolled up its sidewalks long before midnight.

He was scared and he admitted it, telling himself that the only thing really capable of giving him the shakes was a bullet in the back from the darkness. Someone had trailed him after he'd left the drugstore, stalking him through the night the way a hunter would stalk a wild animal, maybe the same man who had shot Old Mike from the ridge.

There was no protection from that kind of thing. Courage? A fast gun? A pair of fists? No good. It was like being struck by lightning. There was nothing you could do if it hit you.

He tried to stay awake, to think back over what had happened in an effort to discover if he had any clue that would lead him to the man who had been trailing him, but he could not think of anything. Then he wondered why the man hadn't fired when he'd whirled his horse and ridden straight at him? He'd better stay awake, he thought. The door had a flimsy lock that could be broken easily enough.

Charlie Gilbert was here in the hotel. Maybe by now he had heard about Lud. It could have been Pete Matts, Whitey's father, but he doubted if Whitey knew who had slugged him. Sid Kehoe? Maybe. Hell, it could have been any of a dozen men who hated Old Mike, and thought that the best way to pull the old man's fang was to kill his son.

In time weariness overcame his fear and he dropped off to sleep, but it wasn't a sound sleep. He turned often, the bed squeaking with each turn. A dog barked from somewhere near the western edge of town. A heavy-footed man walked along the hall past Bill's door. Suddenly two tomcats erupted into a fight on the roof of the building next to the hotel with horrible, spine-tingling caterwauling.

A period of silence followed the cat fight, and, when Bill woke again, it seemed he was completely awake all at once, every nerve alert, a warning tugging at his spine like the humming of a fine, tight wire. Someone was in the room with him, but the door hadn't been smashed open. The intruder must have come through the window, then, and he must have used a ladder, for Bill's room was on the second floor.

A faint gleam of star shine showed at the window. Bill lay on his right side, his arm under him. His gun was in the holster on the floor directly below his head, but any kind of move would set the bed to squeaking. He could not see the man, but he caught the sibilance of his breathing, and then the soft sound of a foot being carefully lowered to the floor.

Bill drew his right arm out from under him, the bed squeaking as he knew it would. All sound stopped for a moment, then a foot came down again. Bill had no way of knowing whether the man had a gun or a knife in his hand. He would certainly have some kind of weapon, and he would have ample time to use it before Bill could paw around in the darkness, locate his gun, and jerk it from leather.

It took all his willpower to lie there and wait, but he had to, not being sure exactly where the man was or what he intended to do. Apparently he had moved around the edge of the room. Now he was close, just about in front of the door, Bill thought, and he knew he could not wait any longer.

He rolled off the bed, hitting the floor hard just as the intruder brought his hand down in a slashing blow with a knife that sliced through the blankets and into the mattress. Bill had him by the legs and brought him down. They rolled over and over, striking with knees and elbow and fists.

The man was slender, but he was wiry and strong, and once he broke free and started toward the window. Bill caught him by an ankle and tripped him, but he couldn't move fast enough to pin him down. The intruder regained his feet, not trying for the window this time but charging at Bill, the top of his head butting Bill under the chin and sending him floundering back toward the door, a galaxy of stars rushing in front of him.

He stumbled across his gun belt. He bent, yanked the gun from the holster, and threw a shot at the man as he went out through the window. He missed, knowing that only by blind luck would he have scored a hit in the darkness. He rushed across the room and leaned out of the window. The top of the ladder was just below the window ledge. He grabbed the top rung and threw the ladder away from the window, but the man was almost down so the fall was not damaging.

Bill heard the ladder hit the ground, then the man's steps as he scurried toward the alley. In the darkness Bill could see nothing, but he fired twice at the sound of the pounding feet. The roar of the shots seemed tremendous in the night silence. Someone pounded on his door. He crossed the room, turned the key, and opened the door.

The hotel owner stood in the hall. "What happened, Varney?"

Others were poking their heads out of doorways, staring at Bill. A couple of south mesa ranchers, a cowhand from the north end of the county, a drummer, and Annie Bain whose face held none of the pleasant expression he had seen the night he and Shaniko Red had eaten supper in the Hell Hole. She hated him just as Charlie Gilbert must hate him, and he thought she wanted him to know it. Gilbert wasn't in sight, and Bill wondered about it. But the intruder hadn't been Charlie Gilbert. Charlie was too big, and he had a bullet-ripped arm.

"What happened?" the hotel man repeated. "Want me to get Grant?"

"No, go to bed," Bill said. "A man came through the window and he went out the same way."

He shut the door and turned the lock, then he lit the lamp, and pulled the knife out of the mattress. A long, shiny blade, razor-sharp, with a pearl handle. It told him nothing, for he had seen a number of knives like it, or similar to it, in Nider's store. He blew out the lamp and went back to bed, but he did not sleep until daylight came. Later, when he got up, he saw that the ladder was gone.

CHAPTER SIXTEEN

Bill had breakfast in the dining room and went immediately to Marian's house. He knew he was early, but he had to get home, and he wanted to see Marian before he left. He wasn't sure he could say anything he hadn't said the last time he'd talked to her. He wasn't sure he could change her mind, but he had to try. Even if she wouldn't marry him, maybe he could keep her from marrying Phil Nider.

His life had changed the instant the dry gulcher's bullet had cut down Old Mike—his immediate future, at least. He wasn't leaving Pitchfork. He'd run the outfit as long as the old man was laid up. Maybe he could stop trouble with the south mesa ranchers. But what about the months ahead after Old Mike was back in the saddle, giving the orders and raising hell again?

Well, he didn't know. Marian would ask. She had a right to. No woman could be expected to marry a man who could see ahead for only a few weeks. Then, as he thought about it, he wasn't sure he was right. If a woman loved a man, and had faith in him, she'd marry him even if she couldn't see past tomorrow. At least that was the way he thought it ought to be.

As Bill walked up the path, he saw that Mrs. Tracey wasn't in her rocking chair on the front porch. Probably still in bed. Marian opened the door to his knock, and stood staring at him in consternation. She was wearing an old faded robe, her toes poking through her slippers, and her hair was down her back.

"Oh, Bill," she said. "I didn't want you to ever see me like this."

"I'm sorry," he said. "It doesn't make any difference. I had to talk to you before I left town."

"Come in," she said resignedly, and led the way through the cluttered workroom to the kitchen. "I was just getting breakfast. Ma's still in bed. She likes to have a cup of coffee before she comes to the table." Embarrassed, she put a hand on the back of a chair. "I was up late last night working on Missus Burnham's dress, and I slept later this morning than I intended to."

"It's my fault. I shouldn't have come so early. You heard about Dad?"

"Just that he'd been shot. How is he?"

"I haven't seen him, but Doc figures he'll make it. That's why I came by here. I've got to get on home." He told her what had happened, leaving nothing out except the attempt on his life in the hotel room. Then he said: "I asked you to marry me and you turned me down. I was aiming to leave the country when Dad was shot, but now I'm staying. I'll make a home for you. I don't know just how, but I will, and we'll figure something out for your mother. I want you to wait for me, Marian."

He felt her stiffen as she backed away from him. He hurried on. "Is it too much to ask, for you to wait a little while?" She said nothing, and he thought of all the time he had wasted when he had not been sure of his feelings. She had been waiting for him to ask her to marry him, but now that he had, she was resisting him. "Marian, I love you. I want you to marry me. Don't you understand?"

"Bill, don't," she whispered. "I can't. I promised Phil Nider."

He stood there, breathing hard, fighting the bitter words that begged to be spoken. Phil Nider with his money and big house and the position of importance he could give her. She'd be equal to Mrs. Frank Burnham. Maybe that was what she wanted; maybe love didn't really mean anything to her.

He was too angry to talk, too hurt, and he wheeled and stalked to the door. Then he stopped. He couldn't give up this easily. He turned and walked back to her.

"All right," he said, "you don't love me, but whatever you do, don't marry Phil Nider. He's old enough to be your father. Maybe your grandfather. He was in love with my mother and wanted her to leave the country with him. Did you know that?"

"I've heard the gossip," she said, "but that was a long time ago. It's got nothing to do with Phil and me. I couldn't see that there was any chance for us, Bill, with Old Mike the way he is and my mother the way she is. Phil understands. He won't expect much from me."

"But you don't love him. You're throwing your life away on an old man. He might live for thirty years. By the time he died, you'd be middle-aged."

She put a hand to her throat. Her face was very pale. He saw the pulse beat in her temples, and he barely heard her voice: "Don't make it any harder for me, Bill. Please. I promised Phil, and I can't break my word as long as he wants me."

He didn't move. He heard Mrs. Tracey's demanding voice calling for her coffee. Marian poured a cup and left the kitchen. Suddenly it occurred to Bill that he was in the same position Shaniko Red was. He loved Vida but he had no chance because she was engaged to Turk Allen.

Then Bill remembered what Shaniko had said, that he'd kill Turk before he'd let Vida marry him. Not that he ever had any hope of marrying Vida. He simply understood Turk better than she did, so he knew what Turk would do to her.

But it was different with Marian. Phil Nider was no Turk Allen. He wouldn't abuse her. He wouldn't make her happy, but apparently she didn't want to be happy. Maybe she knew what she was doing.

When she came back to the kitchen, she said: "I guess you'd better go, Bill. We're just making it harder for each other."

Was he more to blame, he asked himself, because he had waited so long, or was Marian because she was bound to sell herself to Phil Nider so she could quit making dresses and wouldn't have to worry about the store bill and the rent?

He put his arms around her. He said: "You're wrong, Marian. You'll live your whole life knowing it."

He kissed her. For a moment she resisted him, tight fists beating at him, and then all the resistance went out of her. She clung to him, her eyes shut, her arms wrapped tightly around him. There was this moment when she seemed terrified by the thought that she would lose him, this moment when she was impelled to seek refuge in his arms, but when he let her go, asking—"Change your mind?"—she said—"No."—and turned her back to him.

"You'll remember that kiss as long as you live," he said, "and, if you're married to Phil Nider a hundred years, he'll never kiss you like that."

He strode out of the room and on out of the house, and, mounting, left town at a gallop. Presently he pulled his horse down and rode home slowly, the violence of his feelings blunted by the knowledge that he had failed. She was the kind of woman who would keep her word no matter what it cost her just as she would go on taking care of her mother no matter what that cost her. He should respect her for her integrity, but he didn't. Integrity, carried this far, seemed to him to be stupidity.

He reached Pitchfork in midmorning and put his horse away. Turk Allen was gone with the crew. Bill didn't much care either way. Firing Turk would be a dirty job, no matter when he did it. He was afraid of Vida more than Turk. He didn't want to turn her against him, but he believed she'd get over it in time. With her there was no question of integrity as there was with Marian, and he was highly doubtful that she had any real love for the man.

The house was very quiet when he went in. He crossed the big living room to the door of Old Mike's bedroom. Vida sat in a rocking chair at the head of the bed. The shades were down, so the room was quite dark, and a moment passed before Bill made out the motionless figure of his father on the bed. He lay on his back, asleep, his mouth open.

Vida glanced up and saw Bill, then rose and walked to him. She asked in a fretful voice: "Where have you been?"

He backed into the living room. Vida closed the door behind her. Now, out in the light, he saw that she looked more tired than he had realized.

"You been with him since he was shot?" he asked.

She nodded. "Except when I was in the kitchen fixing some broth for him." She sat down on the leather couch. "I can't remember any of us being sick since we were kids. Not Dad, anyway. Doc says he'll make it, but I don't know. I'm afraid it'll kill him just to lie in bed and Doc says he'll be there for weeks."

She put her head against the back of the couch, her legs extended before her, utterly relaxed now that Bill was here. She had gone without sleep for more than twenty-four hours, and she looked it.

"Shaniko would have sat up with Dad," Bill said.

"I didn't feel like asking him," she said. "I did ask Turk, but he wouldn't do it."

She said it bitterly. The first time she had ever used that tone in Bill's presence when she was talking about Turk. He asked: "Why wouldn't he?"

"He said he wasn't any good as a nurse." Her lips tightened. "Bill, I don't understand him. He acted as if he hoped Dad would die. He didn't do it, did he?"

"No," Bill said, and, sitting down beside her, told her what he had done. "Maybe it wasn't Lud, but it must have been somebody Lud knew and trusted. He sure wouldn't have anything to do with Turk."

"No, I guess not," Vida said. "You don't have any idea who tried to kill you last night?"

"Sid Kehoe, maybe. That'd be about his size, and he's not one to forget I killed his brother."

"Trouble," she said resentfully. "It will be worse if you leave. Are you still going to?"

"No."

"I'm glad. I didn't want you to, but I didn't think there was any use to ask you to stay. Bill, I've done a lot of thinking since we brought Dad in yesterday morning. Didn't have anything else to do but just sit there beside the bed and try to get him to eat a little broth when he was awake. I asked myself why he's treated you the way he has and why he didn't get along with Mamma? And what has it got him, living the way he has and making everybody knuckle under? But I couldn't think of any answers. Just questions."

Her voice was low and without expression. He wondered why she had said the things she had. Maybe it was just because she was tired, or maybe she was seeing things a little differently now. But one thing was sure, and the thought brought him satisfaction. Turk Allen had made a bad mistake when he'd refused to sit up with Old Mike.

"Why don't you go to bed?" he asked. "I'll take my turn sitting with him."

"I guess I'd better," she said, "or I'll drop over on my face. There's some broth on the stove you can give him if he's hungry. You can find something to eat in the pantry."

"When did Turk show up?"

She started toward her room. She turned, and again her voice was bitter. "I'm not sure. As soon as Birnie fetched the doctor, he rode off. When he came back, Turk was with him. It was some time in the afternoon."

She went into her room and shut the door. She didn't know what was going on, he thought, but she was beginning to wonder. In time she'd get the right answers. One thing still bothered him. He'd have to kill Turk, or beat him so badly he'd leave. Turk figured he was too solid with Old Mike and Vida to take his walking papers from Bill. What would Vida do then? He didn't know, but he was afraid.

He sat down beside Old Mike's bed. Near noon his father stirred and finally woke. He recognized Bill, but he didn't ask any questions. Bill brought him a bowl of broth and Old Mike got most of it down. After that, he lay there, his eyes open, but saying nothing. Bill warmed up some leftovers he found in the pantry and returned to Old Mike's room.

"I thought you were leaving," the old man said.

"Changed my mind."

"You get the bastard that shot me?"

"No."

"Didn't figure you would. You took after your ma, not me."

That was like him. Lying here with a bullet hole in him, he ran true to form. Bill could hate him, for this and all the other injustices he had suffered over the years, and he wondered if Marian hated her mother the same way. No, probably not. Their problems were much the same, but there was a difference. Mrs. Tracey was a clinger, and Old Mike had pushed Bill away as long as Bill could remember.

In late afternoon Vida woke and came into the bedroom. Bill said: "He's been asleep for quite a spell."

"Get some wood," Vida said. "I'll sit with him."

"Doc coming out this evening?"

"He promised to."

Bill chopped enough wood for supper and breakfast. When

he finished, he saw the crew riding down the ridge behind the house. He carried the wood into the kitchen, then returned to the porch and checked his gun. Better that Vida didn't know about this until it was over, he decided, and crossed the yard to the corral. There he waited.

CHAPTER SEVENTEEN

Dutch John had been riding beside Turk Allen. When he saw Bill, he dropped back to ride with Shaniko Red and Birnie Hanks, leaving Allen alone in front. That's the way it was, too, Bill thought. Except for Old Mike and Vida, Turk Allen was alone and had been right from the start, but this was the first time any test had been made of the loyalty of the other men.

If Allen felt the flow of hostility from the rest, he gave no indication of it. He was a great block in the saddle, his face filled with his usual good humor. As always, Bill felt that it was false, a mask he showed the world, particularly to Vida, and only on a few occasions had Bill seen that mask stripped from him

Bill had a feeling Allen knew what was coming. If he did, he plainly had no doubt of his ability to handle the situation. There was an arrogance about him that was real; his half-smiling way of looking at Bill was a gesture of royal contempt. He wasn't afraid. His failure to ride in the morning Old Mike was shot did not indicate fear. Rather, it was typical of his way of doing things. This clash with Bill was something he would have avoided if possible simply because he had little to gain and a great deal to lose.

Now that the clash was at hand, Allen did not back away from it. He reined up, saying affably: "So you didn't pull out after all. I had the notion you were shaking the dust of the old homestead from your feet."

"Don't take the saddle off your horse," Bill said. "Pack your war sack and get to hell off the ranch."

Allen stepped down, laughing. "That's big talk, boy. It'll take a man to fire me, a man like Old Mike." The others had dismounted and Allen handed the reins of his horse to Birnie Flanks. "Take care of him. I'm going in to see how the old man is."

"You're not going anywhere except off Pitchfork," Bill said. "You're fired. Have I got to write you a letter?"

"Why, sonny, I didn't know you could write." Allen cuffed his Stetson back on his forehead. "Strikes me kind o' funny, you sashaying around over the country while your dad was lying in bed, all shot to hell. You didn't think enough of him to stay here and see how he made out." He shrugged his massive shoulders. "But I reckon Old Mike didn't expect it, you being the kind of hairpin you are."

Allen started toward the house. Bill said: "You take three more steps and my gun will be smoking."

Allen wheeled, the good humor wiped from his face. "Well, by God, you bother a man just like a gnat in his ear. You can't fire me and you know it."

"I can sure give you a chunk of lead to chew on. Long as Dad's laid up, I'm running the outfit, and I'm starting by firing you."

"I ain't swapping smoke with you, sonny," Allen said. "Old Mike might fire me if I burned you down." He motioned at Shaniko. "Get your gun on him so he won't do nothing foolish."

"Not me," Shaniko said. "I figure you're in for a whipping. You've had one coming for a long time."

"A whipping, is it?" Allen snapped, and stripped off his gun belt. "Somebody's gonna get one, but it ain't me. I've stood all this gab I'm going to."

Bill jerked off his gun belt and tossed it toward the corral. He was rid of it barely in time. Allen was on him, both fists swinging. They met with a savage impact, Bill catching him in his middle with a hard right. But it took more than that to stop Allen. The impetus of his charge carried Bill back toward the corral. He stepped aside, whipping another right to the side of Allen's head. The blow sent him sprawling into the yard dust. He got up, swearing, and drove at Bill again, his dignity hurt more than anything else.

Bill stood his ground and they traded blow for blow, the sound of fist on hard muscle and bone like that of a maul driving a post into the ground. Allen had no liking for this kind of fighting. Bill was the taller with longer arms, and he kept his man back on his heels, hurting him, while Allen's blows didn't land with full authority.

Suddenly Allen backed up and then, reversing himself, drove at Bill, bent over in a crouch, his arms reaching out to grip Bill by the legs and drag him down. It didn't work. Bill, sensing this maneuver, brought his knee up squarely into Allen's face, a wicked blow that snapped his head back and put him into the dust a second time.

From what seemed a great distance Bill heard Vida screaming at him. He turned to see her running toward him from the house. He looked back at Allen, but he was too late. Allen hadn't been hurt as much as Bill had thought. This time the foreman got him by the knees and succeeded in bringing him down. They rolled over and over in the dust, fighting like two schoolboys at recess.

This was Turk Allen's kind of fighting. He could and did use his greater strength and weight to an advantage. He batted Bill in the face with his head, used his fists and elbows against Bill's ribs, tried to knee him in the crotch and almost succeeded. Through the grunting and panting and the ringing in his head,

Bill heard Vida's screams, and Shaniko and Birnie Hanks and Dutch John yelling at him to get on his feet.

They rolled over again. Bill, on top now, slammed his head down on Allen's nose, flattening it, blood spurting in a red stream. Bill got free and rolled away and gained his feet. Allen, on his hands and knees, looked up at Bill, dazed for a moment, then came on up, wiped a sleeve across his nose, and drove at Bill again.

Bill backed up until he stood against the corral gate. He wheeled aside and again they faced each other, slugging, trading long, punishing blows. No sound now except the thud of striking fists and grunts and labored breathing.

A sort of savage exultation was in Bill. He wished Old Mike could see this. He should have whipped Turk a long time ago; he should have stood up for himself against Old Mike, and then ridden off the way he had intended to do yesterday. But it was too late for that. This was now, and he felt pleasure as he drove blow after blow to Allen's middle or his head, the jar coming on up his arm to his shoulder.

He thought he had Allen licked when a punch came through that he didn't see in time. He went down. Allen kicked him brutally in the ribs. Vida screamed and Shaniko yelled a warning at the foreman. Then Bill was up again, his head ringing.

Allen charged like a berserk bull, head down, intending to ram Bill in the belly. Bill turned aside and brought a fist in a hard, down-driving blow across the back of Allen's neck. The foreman sprawled on the ground, face plowing through the dirt, and lay on his stomach, out cold.

Bill leaned against the corral gate and sucked great gulps of air into his lungs. Vida cried: "Let me go! Let me go!" Bill wiped a hand across his face. It came away wet with blood and sweat. Then he saw that Shaniko had been holding Vida in front of him, one arm around her, the other hand gripping both wrists behind her.

When Shaniko released Vida, she ran to Bill, crying out: "Are you hurt, Bill?"

He was starved for breath. He hurt in a dozen places, and blood kept trickling down his face as fast as he could wipe it off, but he could never remember a moment in his life that gave him the deep, sweet pleasure this did. She had come to him, her brother, not the man she was supposed to marry.

"Sure, I'm all right," he said. "I thought it was Turk you were worried about."

She started to cry. She put her arms around him and laid her head against his chest. "Bill, Bill," she said, "it took this to show me I'd been wrong. I was afraid he'd kill you. Then when he kicked you in the ribs. . . ."

She couldn't go on. Bill motioned to Shaniko. "Get him on his feet and into the saddle."

Shaniko and Dutch John pulled Allen to his feet and, dragging him to the horse trough, shoved his head into it time after time until he came around, snorting and pawing at his face. They pushed him across the yard to his horse and got him into the saddle. Birnie handed him his gun belt.

"We'll send your stuff to town and you can pick it up at the Stockade," Bill said. "I'll see Burnham. and you get what you've got coming from the bank."

Allen sat his saddle like a sack of wool, one hand gripping the horn, slumped over, blood still dripping from his nose. He said: "You're going to stand for this, Vida?"

She had stepped away from Bill, her strong, tanned face the picture of defiance. "I'll stand for it, all right," she said. "I never want to see you again."

He was too dazed to think straight, but this got through to him. He asked: "You mean that?"

"I never meant anything more in my life," she said. "Get off Pitchfork. Don't come back."

He rode away, hunched over, still holding onto the horn.

Shaniko said: "He'll be back. He ain't one to forget."

Birnie Hanks handed Bill his gun belt. He buckled it on, crossed to the horse trough, and dipped his head into the water. He straightened up and rubbed his face with his hands. He said: "I want to see you, Shaniko." He started toward the house. Vida was beside him. He asked: "What changed you?"

"I don't know, Bill," she said slowly. "I thought I could stop it when I went out there. If Shaniko hadn't grabbed me, I'd have got hurt. Then I had to watch it. I guess I didn't really know how I felt until he kicked you in the side, and then I hated him."

She was silent for a time. When they reached the porch, she said: "Maybe I never loved him. I was too stubborn to listen to you or Shaniko. The more you talked against him, the more I was bound to marry him. He was the kind of foreman Dad wanted. Maybe that had something to do with it."

Bill pulled himself up to the porch by holding onto a post, then lowered himself into a rocking chair. Vida said: "You knew what he was, didn't you?"

"I've told you often enough," he said. "You'd have been in hell, married to him."

"How did you know?"

"I've seen him handle horses and men. He'd do the same to a woman who belonged to him."

That seemed to satisfy her. She said: "I'll go sit with Dad."

He stayed on the porch, watching Turk Allen until he disappeared over the edge of the mesa hill. Shaniko was right. Allen would be back. But how? And when? There was no way to know, nothing to do but wait.

CHAPTER EIGHTEEN

The clouds had broken away during the day, but they had gathered again. The air was motionless and sultry. Lightning crackled above the western horizon, and the rumble of distant thunder reminded Bill that the storm that had been gathering when he'd been at Horn's place was still on the way. He wondered if it would come that night. Maybe the attack that Phil Nider and Ed Grant had warned him about would come that night, too.

He rolled and lit a cigarette, took a few puffs, and threw it away. There was no pleasure in it, his mouth battered as it was. Maybe he should have sent to the Flat Tops for help, then decided it was too far. If the attack came tonight, the reinforcements would be too late, and he would be one man weaker. There were four of them, five with Vida. She could shoot with the best of them. She would, too. There was that much of Old Mike in her.

Shaniko appeared, grinning a little as he said: "What's on your mind, boss?"

"Cut it out," Bill said testily. "I've always been Bill to you. I aim to keep it that way."

"You done quite a job. How do you feel?"

"Like a piece of sausage that just came through the grinder."

"What do you suppose Turk feels like?"

"I don't much care," Bill said. "I'm a lot more interested in what he's going to do."

144

"I've been wondering. If Vida hadn't given him his walking papers, I'd say he'd stay in town till Old Mike got on his feet, but, the way it is, I'm guessing he'll throw in with Charlie Gilbert and Sid Kehoe and the rest. That's his size."

Vida appeared in the doorway. "Dad wants to see you, Bill."

There'd be hell to pay now, Bill thought as he got up and went into the old man's bedroom. The light was thin inside the house, and Vida touched a match to the lamp on the bureau as Bill came through the door. Old Mike was fully conscious. He was pale, but his eyes were bright as they always were when he was in one of his rages.

"What the hell is this about you picking a fight with Turk?" Old Mike demanded.

"I'll get your broth," Vida said.

"I don't want no damned broth," the old man said angrily. "You stay here and listen."

"You're not going to get well if you stay steamed up like this," Bill said. "I'm running Pitchfork as long as you're laid up, and you'll stay laid up if you keep acting this way."

"By God, I asked you a question. You gonna answer . . . ?"

"I didn't pick a fight. I fired him and he didn't like it."

"You fired him, did you? Now who gave you any authority to fire Turk? He's foreman. Not you." Old Mike motioned to Vida. "Go to town and get him. I'll show this young pup who's running Pitchfork."

"No," Vida said. "I'll never bring Turk here. If he does come back, Bill will kill him."

Old Mike blinked, puzzled by Vida's outburst, his gaze moving to Bill and back to Vida. "Have both of you been drinking panther milk? I don't savvy this."

"Nothing to savvy," Bill said. "You're going to be laid up for a long time. Somebody's got to run this outfit and it looked to me like I was it. Turk was the biggest liability we had, so I got

145

rid of him."

"Why?" Old Mike demanded. "He's the best damned fore-man on Skull River and you ain't dry behind the ears."

"I'm drying up fast," Bill said. "You've never been able to see anything you didn't want to see. You thought Turk was hell on high red wheels because he'd do your dirty work and keep people afraid of him and drive a crew till their tails were drag-ging. But it takes more'n that to make a good ramrod."

Old Mike ignored him and turned his gaze to Vida. "What changed you? You were going to marry him. What happened?"

"Let's say I got my eyes open," she said. "I guess I never loved him. I tried to make myself go ahead with it because you wanted me to, but when he didn't come back after they burned Charlie Gilbert out, I thought he was hurt. He wasn't, and he didn't give any reason for waiting until afternoon to ride in with Birnie. Then this evening, when Bill was down, he kicked him. Well, I guess I just saw the kind of man he was."

"Hell, you knowed all the time. Turk never tried to cover up what he was."

"Then maybe it was because I understood you for the first time," she said. "The way you acted when Bill kept Ace Kehoe from killing you. And when he was going to leave, you didn't try to stop him. You've always had to run everything, and I've let you run me because I love you, but I don't love you enough to marry Turk Allen. There's too much of you in me. In Bill, too. That's why he finally made up his mind to leave."

"Bill? Hell, he's always been soft. Like his mother."

"Soft?" Vida said. "You think it took a soft man to kill Ace Kehoe? To run Lud Gilbert down and kill him? To lick Turk today?" She shook her head. "No, he's not soft. You know what I think? I believe you've known all the time he wasn't soft and you've been afraid of him."

Old Mike closed his eyes, and he looked tired and old and

sick. Bill, watching him, sensed that what Vida said was true. His father had been afraid of him, afraid Bill would challenge him just as he was doing now.

"Looks like I've lived too long," Old Mike said. "I should have died the day your mother wanted to leave me to go to Phil Nider. It was a long time ago, but that was when I should have died. I've wanted to a dozen times since then. I wanted Kehoe to kill me. I guess this is the wind-up, and now that it's here, I don't give a good god damn."

"No," Vida said. "If you behave yourself, you'll live a long time."

He was silent, then asked in a tired voice: "What are you fixing to do, Bill, now that you're 'rodding Pitchfork?"

"I'm going to try to get some peace on this range," he said. "Promise 'em we're satisfied. Tell 'em we're not going across the river like they think we are. If they jump us tonight, there's not much I can do, but, if they wait, I'll try to talk some sense into 'em."

"You keep growing or you die," the old man said. "That's why I've done what I have."

"You're wrong, Dad," Bill said. "If you keep pushing, they'll push back, sooner or later."

"They'll never push anything," he said contemptuously. "They're a bunch of scared old women. Vida, fetch me that broth."

Bill left the room with Vida. He lit the bracket lamp in the kitchen and pulled the shades as she poured broth from the pan into a bowl. She looked at Bill, trying to smile, but not quite managing it.

"Funny," she said. "We're twins, but we aren't much alike. Lately we haven't even understood each other very well. It's different now. I guess I began to see it when I went to the line cabin and you promised to fight Kehoe. After you did and Dad

147

acted the way he did, well, all of a sudden I saw he was a little man, Bill, just a little, greedy old man."

"You think he's really afraid of me?"

"Yes, I'm sure of it. That's why he never gave you a chance to do anything. I think there's something else, too. It was his way of getting at Mamma. You did take after her, you know."

"Then why has he been bound to Turk the way he has? He should have been afraid of him, too."

She shook her head. "No, he could handle Turk. I think he's always known the day would come when he couldn't handle you."

"You think he meant it when he said he wanted Kehoe to kill him?"

"Maybe he did. He's never been happy. Not as long as I can remember. I was in the house a lot more than you were, so I understood how it was between him and Mamma better than you do. She froze him out, Bill. They were like two strangers. She was a girl when they were married and he was over forty. Maybe that had something to do with it."

She took the broth to Old Mike and Bill left the house to eat supper with the crew in the cook shack. When they were done, he said: "We may have trouble tonight, so we'll keep a guard out. Shaniko 'n' me will take it till midnight." He nodded at Dutch John. "You 'n' Birnie can handle it the rest of the night. We'll move all the guns and shells we've got into the house. No sense trying to defend all the buildings."

Shaniko's mournful face seemed longer than ever. "May be a long night," he said.

Dutch John slapped him on the back. "We'll wait till sunup to bury you."

Birnie Hanks, his eyes bright with anticipation, said: "If they show up around here, they'll wish they hadn't."

"Soon Hee," Bill said to the Chinese cook, "if there's trouble, you get into the house. You'll lose your pigtail if they catch you."

Soon Hee flourished a meat cleaver. "Me fight velly good."

"Sure, you're a hell of a fighter," Bill said. When he was outside, he told Shaniko: "I'll bet Soon Hee will take off for the ridge with the first shot."

"He'll stop some lead if he does," Shaniko said.

They carried their guns to the front room of the house, laid the rifles on the oak table, and spread their ammunition beside the rifles. They were filling the loops of their gun belts when Dr. Ripple drove up in his buggy and came in.

He nodded when he saw the guns and set his black bag on a chair. "You'll need them before morning. There's a dozen of 'em in town. They've been having a meeting in Phil Nider's store. Charlie Gilbert seems to be leading them. I tried to talk to them. So did Ed Grant, but, hell, we might just as well have saved our wind. When men get worked up to the place they are, they aren't men any more. They're animals. Like wolves following their leader."

"That'd be Charlie Gilbert," Bill said.

"Well, I reckon so." Ripple stroked his beard, frowning. "Bill, it's a funny thing. I said it seems to be Gilbert, but I've got a hunch Phil Nider's the one who keeps fanning the flames. All of us know how he feels about Old Mike, but this is the first time he's actually come out and taken a stand." He picked up his bag. "Well, I'll take a look at your dad and head back for town."

"No use for me to go to bed," Birnie said. "I won't sleep none."

"You try," Bill said. "It'll be a long night, all right."

He went outside with Shaniko. Dutch John and Birnie went on to the bunkhouse. The doctor came out a few minutes later. Bill asked: "How is he?"

"Tired," Ripple answered. "Vida told me he got pretty worked up a while ago, but he'll be all right. Takes more than one slug to get him. Well, I've got to get wheeling. I promised Marian I'd see her mother tonight. All she needs is somebody to gab to." He stepped into the buggy. "Bill, how many men have you got on the Flat Tops?"

"Eight. Why?"

"Ed Grant went after them. I told him he'd better come out here, but he thinks it'll be tomorrow night before they get up enough nerve to make their fight. If Nider and the rest of them know you had a dozen men here, they won't come. Trouble is, Ed went too late. He should have gone yesterday. Or you should have."

"No," Bill said. "Most of our cattle are on the Flat Tops. They need looking after. We can't spend our summer playing like we're an army garrison."

"You think four of you can fight off all them south mesa boys?"

Ripple snorted his derision and drove away. The sun was down now, dark clouds hanging low, and the smell of rain and sage was strong.

Shaniko came up, saying: "It'll rain before morning. Maybe that'll hold 'em off."

"We'd best not count on it," Bill said. "How do you reckon they'll come?"

"Depends. If Gilbert's leading 'em, they'll come shooting. If it's Nider, they'll sneak in and knife us if they get a chance."

Bill nodded. That was the basic difference in the two men. "You move around on the other side of the barn. I'll take this side. Fire a shot if anything's wrong."

Shaniko grunted his agreement and walked away. The twilight faded, and then the black pressing night was all around them, relieved only by lightning that flashed across the sky and was gone.

Bill settled down to wait. Like Birnie, he knew he would not sleep tonight. If there had to be a fight, he hoped it would come soon. He could not wait through another night. Then he thought sourly that this had been coming for twenty years, and now it was here and Old Mike was safe in bed.

CHAPTER NINETEEN

A sense of failure nagged Phil Nider when he returned home after his abortive attempt to kill Bill Varney in his hotel room. He had moved the ladder back to his store as soon as the hotel quieted down. He had left the knife in the mattress, but it was a common knife that might have been owned by anyone in Broken Nose. The room had been so dark that he felt certain young Varney had not recognized him. He wasn't afraid he would be identified. He simply despised failure.

He took off his clothes and lay on top of the bed, sweating, for even with the window open, the room still held the stagnant heat of the previous day. He had always been a man of precision, a careful planner, coldly efficient, and successful in everything he attempted whether it had been a train robbery in his youth or a business venture since he had come to Broken Nose.

The only failure he could remember had been with Clara Varney, and he blamed Old Mike for that, but he couldn't blame Old Mike for not dying. He simply hadn't shot straight enough. He had only himself to blame for the fact that Bill was still alive, too. Even worse than that was the narrow escape he'd had.

If it got out that he'd tried to knife Bill Varney, he'd lose the respect of everyone who knew him, and that included Marian. You could shoot a man as Bill had shot Ace Kehoe, or even Lud Gilbert, and be considered a brave man, but ambush someone as Nider had tried to do with Old Mike, or knife a man as he'd attempted to do with Bill, and you were a coward and an outcast. A hell of a standard, he thought. It was success that counted, not the way you did the job.

His luck had been bad, but he hadn't been caught, so his luck hadn't been too bad. He had made up his mind that three people were going to die, and, by God, they would. He'd take care of Mrs. Tracey. It would be simple enough when Marian was gone to choir practice.

He had taken an unnecessary risk trying to knife Bill and now he wished he hadn't. If he read the sign right, Charlie Gilbert and Sid Kehoe and Pete Matts and their friends would take care of Old Mike and Bill, and he wouldn't be involved at all. He wouldn't even have to do much prodding when Charlie heard about Lud.

He went to sleep at last, satisfied that things would work out exactly as he wanted them to. He was desperately tired, for he had slept very little the night before. It was 10:00 A.M. when he awoke. He shaved and dressed with feverish haste, bitterly condemning himself for not waking at his regular hour, and knowing it might prove a fatal mistake. Above all things, he wanted this day to appear perfectly normal.

In spite of Mrs. O'Toole's protests, he didn't wait for breakfast, but hurried to the store, nodded at Carl Akins, and went on back to his office. He tried to work on his books, but he had trouble keeping his mind on his business. Precisely at 12:00 he left the store, went home to dinner, and returned at 1:00. This much at least followed the pattern of an ordinary day.

Horses were racked along the street, and knots of men stood in front of the hotel and the Stockade and the bank. He thought of leaving the store to talk to them, and decided against it. He stood behind a window, staring at the men in the street while

Akins was home for dinner. The storm was gathering without any help from him. It was in their faces; it was a feeling and a smell in the air. A long time coming, but it was here at last, and he wouldn't have to lift a finger.

But late in the afternoon he found the storm swirling around his head, and in a manner he had not expected. He was waiting on a customer and Akins was working in the back room when Charlie Gilbert led the procession into the store. A dozen or more, Sid Kehoe following Gilbert, then Pete Matts, with the rest strung out behind. They waited until Nider finished with his customer, silent, angry men, all of them armed, the look of death on their bitter faces. Nider moved along the counter to them, asking: "What'll it be, gents?"

"We want to meet in your back room," Gilbert said. "My hotel room's too small. Hotter'n hell, too."

Gilbert was a mountain of a man, his left arm in a sling, his face drawn and gray, his eyes bitter. Nider's gaze swept the men behind Gilbert, indecision holding him silent for a moment. This would force him into their stall, but it didn't make any difference. He was there anyway.

"Sure," Nider said, "but looks to me like the Stockade would be a better place."

"You know what Chauncey Morts is," Gilbert said. "We figure you're on our side, judging by what you said to me the other day. You are, aren't you?"

"I'm not on Old Mike Varney's side," Nider said quickly, still putting off the commitment he knew he would have to make sooner or later.

He led the way to the back room, motioning for Carl Akins to leave. As soon as all of them were in the room, he closed the door. They sat down on boxes and crates and kegs, Gilbert standing in the middle beside an unopened cracker barrel. He was like a wounded bear, his mind on one thing. With Gilbert leading them, Nider thought, they'd tear Pitchfork apart.

"How far are you going with us, Nider?" Gilbert asked.

"I don't know what you mean," Nider said carefully. "What are your plans?"

"We're going to burn Pitchfork just like they burned the Hell Hole," Gilbert said. "You warned us, but you didn't have the right hunch. Maybe you double-crossed us. On the other hand, maybe you didn't know."

"I didn't double-cross you, damn it," Nider snapped. "I told you what I'd heard. That was all I knew. It wasn't my fault you got burned out."

"All right," Pete Matts said. "Maybe it wasn't, but they made fools out of us. Tonight it's going to be different. So far you've straddled the fence. Now we're aiming to get both your feet on our side."

Gilbert nodded. "Everybody else in town is on Varney's side. We need somebody on ours. I ain't leaving the country, Nider. I'm gonna have me a saloon right here in town and I'll run Chauncey Morts out of business. With Old Mike dead, you'll throw as much weight around as anybody. Maybe more. I've even heard talk you was interested in getting hold of Pitchfork."

Nider chewed on his lower lip, knowing that the rumor had come from Frank Burnham. He hadn't mentioned his ambition to anyone else, and the only reason he'd talked to the banker about it was to find out how much Old Mike was in debt. With the price of beef down, he was in a squeeze. If Nider could buy up his notes, he'd be in position to tighten that squeeze. But he didn't like a rumor of this sort going around. It was his business and his only, exactly as his reason for hating Old Mike was his.

"My interests are not open to discussion," Nider said. "I still don't savvy what you're getting at."

"You're going to take a stand," Gilbert said. "Now. Are you on our side or on Varney's? If you're on ours, how far will you go with us?"

"I'll furnish you with guns and ammunition," he said. "I don't see any sense in my riding with you tonight. I'm a storekeeper, and I'm not very familiar with guns."

"We'll need some rifles and shells, all right," Gilbert said, "but that ain't enough. We don't need you with us tonight. I reckon we can do the job. It's tomorrow we're thinking about. Ed Grant is Varney's man. . . ."

He stopped. The door from the store had opened and Ed Grant and Dr. Ripple came in.

Gilbert said: "Get out. This is a closed meeting."

"Then it's time you were opening it up to a little horse sense," Grant said. "I've heard the talk all day. You're going to burn Pitchfork. I'm here to warn you. I'll jail every one of you if you do it, and you'll go to Canon City for twenty years."

Pete Matts jumped up and shook his fist at Grant. "Anybody going to Canon City for burning Charlie out? Or for shooting Lud? Or for cracking my boy's head? If he dies, it's murder. You fixing to arrest anybody, Sheriff?"

"If you know who done it, I'll arrest him and he'll be tried," Grant said. "Gilbert, you claim it was Pitchfork that burned you out, but you never saw anybody and you can't swear it was them. What you're doing is open and shut. You're even bragging about what you're aiming to do. I'd have to arrest you."

"You won't be arresting nobody," Gilbert said. "The law on Skull River has been Varney law. From now on it's going to be our law. I got the dirty end of the stick when I came here. You know what happened. You know a lot of other things that have happened and you've never done a damned thing about it. You and Burnham and Doc and the rest have been on Varney's side right along."

"Now hold on," Ripple said. "You're not talking sense. I'm not on anybody's side."

"The hell you're not," Gilbert snapped. "Anyhow, there's no doubt about the sheriff. I lost my boy. Sid lost his brother. Maybe Pete will lose Whitey. What have you done, Sheriff? Not a god-damned thing. That's why we're gonna run this country from now on. We're starting with Pitchfork. Then we're taking that star off your shirt and we're chasing you down the road so fast your heels will smoke. Maybe we'll burn this stinking town and build our own."

"You'll be dead before then!" Grant shouted. "You go ahead with this and you'll find out what I'll do!"

"Grant, there's one thing you're overlooking," Gilbert said. "We've got one man in this town on our side. He hasn't sucked around after Varney the way the rest of this town has. He's got money. He's respected. He was behind Ace Kehoe coming. He tried to warn us about Pitchfork raiding us, and, if we'd had any sense, we'd have stopped 'em."

Gilbert strode toward Grant, a heavy finger wagging at him. "We're taking over, Sheriff. You're nothing. You won't get anywhere going to the capital and trying to get the governor to interfere." Gilbert laid a hand on Nider's shoulder. "Here's a man who represents the best law-abiding interests on Skull River. He's on our side because he's honest and he knows what's got to be done."

"What about it, Phil?" Ripple demanded. "He's lying, isn't he?"

"You think we'd be here in his back room having our meeting if he wasn't on our side?" Gilbert asked. "One honest man, Doc. That's more than Varney's got on his side."

"I want to hear you say it, Phil," Ripple said. "Not Charlie."

Silence then, with both Grant and Ripple staring at Nider. He could stop it, he thought. For some reason, maybe just because he was considered a law-abiding man, Gilbert's bunch felt they had to have him. But if he stopped it, Old Mike and

Bill Varney would live. So he had no choice.

"I'm with them," Nider said. "We've let Old Mike run over all of us, and now there's not one of us who live in town who can call himself a man. I'm sick of it."

"You've waited a long time for this, haven't you, Phil?" Ripple asked.

"Too long," Nider said, "but this is bigger than my feelings. When Pitchfork gets so big it can raid a man and burn him out without the law doing anything, then it's gone too far."

Grant's face was red. It sounded good, Nider thought. Mighty good. Old Mike's maneuverings were too well known to have this argument refuted. Ed Grant wasn't proud of himself. You could tell that by looking at him.

Sid Kehoe said: "That ain't all, Sheriff. Varney's cleaned off the north side of the river and now he's coming after us. But we ain't waiting."

"And you know why, Grant," Pete Matts said bitterly. "We know you won't protect us, so we'd be fools to wait and get knocked over one at a time."

"Bill Varney talked to me last night," Grant said. "He told me to tell you that he was running Pitchfork and he wasn't coming across the river. Now forget the whole business and go on home."

Nider laughed silently. "Ed, do you think anybody's going to believe you, with Charlie's boy lying in Doc's place, waiting to be buried?"

"I'm warning you," Grant said. "You go ahead and you'll go to jail."

Grant and Ripple walked out of the room. There was a moment of silence after they'd left. This hadn't gone the way Nider had planned, but it was all right. He was in the open. He had been forced to accept it as inevitable and now he did not feel bad about it.

"Let's get the guns you need, boys," Nider said briskly, and opened the door into the store. "Carl, give me a hand."

Later, as he walked home, Nider fell into his old habit of looking ahead and planning. He would never really possess Marian until Old Mike was dead. All of this would be taken care of tonight. Failure and bad luck would not continue to dog his footsteps.

But after tonight? He frowned, realizing he was throwing his weight behind Charlie Gilbert, and Gilbert would be hard to manage. He was no Sid Kehoe or Pete Matts. Well, Gilbert would die the same as any man, and that was probably the only thing that would solve the problem.

Then it would be Phil Nider's town and he'd eventually get hold of Pitchfork just as a matter of personal satisfaction. He'd put Mrs. Burnham in her place, too, and Marian would rule Broken Nose's social life just as he ruled the political and economic side. A long time coming, he thought, but now it was time to move. He found he didn't regret anything that had happened today.

After supper he changed his shirt and strolled through the gathering twilight to Marian's place. A storm was coming up. He liked that. It had been dry and hot too long. And Old Mike Varney had run things too long.

He found Marian quiet and withdrawn, and, when he kissed her, he had the feeling she was far away, that it was her body and not her heart that had been promised to him. Well, she had warned him, but he'd change her feelings. Just give him a little time, and with Bill Varney out of the way, Marian would give her heart to him as well as her body. He waited on the porch until Marian joined him after putting her mother to bed. She said: "I hate to leave Ma alone, but I guess she'll be all right."

"Sure she will," he said. "You won't be gone long." They left the house, Marian's arm through his. She had never walked with him that way. She had made a bargain and she would keep it, he told himself, a better bargain than she had realized when she'd made it.

"It may rain before you get home," he said.

"I'm not made of sugar or salt," she said. "I won't melt."

"Sugar, but not salt," he said gallantly. But she didn't laugh, or even give him a smile, and he sensed the dark mood that possessed her. "I've been too busy to get word to Benjy Combs to fetch that mare to town, but I promise I will tomorrow."

"No hurry, Phil," she said.

Her tone and her words irritated him. She was too cool, too impersonal. After that they walked in silence until they reached the church and he said: "I'll be here to take you home. You wait for me."

"All right, Phil," she said, and went inside.

He strode away, the irritation still nagging him. Maybe she regretted her bargain already, or maybe she'd seen Bill Varney today and he had tried to talk her out of it. To hell with Varney! He wouldn't be talking anyone out of anything by sunup tomorrow.

He went into the store, and, going on back to the office, lit a lamp and pulled the shade down far enough so no one could see he wasn't there, and left the store through the back door. This wouldn't take long. It was dark now, and unless someone happened to catch him in a flash of lightning, he wouldn't be seen.

He followed the alley to a side street, then paused, crouching against the rear wall of a building. Gilbert and Sid Kehoe were on the corner talking to someone, the rest of the men in the street with horses. A match flared to light a cigarette. He saw in surprise that the man talking to Gilbert and Kehoe was Turk Allen.

The match went out, but he could not have mistaken Allen's

160

face. Or his voice as he said: "I'm your man, Charlie. Varney took a club to me today. I ain't one to forget it."

"How many are out there?" Gilbert asked.

"Four of 'em, besides the cook and Old Mike who's flat on his back."

"And Varney's girl?"

"Yeah, she's there. I figure that bastard of a brother of hers is holding her prisoner. She belongs to me. That's all I want out of the deal."

From the front of the livery stable Pete Matts called: "Let's ride!"

Nider didn't move until the band of riders left town headed for Pitchfork. Then he hurried toward the Tracey house, keeping in the shadows. He wasn't quite sure he understood what had happened, but apparently Allen had cut loose from Pitchfork. It was something he could look into later, he thought. Turk Allen was a man he could use.

CHAPTER TWENTY

For Bill Varney the hours before midnight ran on and on without end. He circled the house again and again, stopping often to listen, but he heard nothing except the call of a coyote from the ridge behind the house, or the booming of thunder that came hard on the heels of the lightning flashes.

He could not see anything except when lightning threw its bright, brief light upon the mesa, and, when it did, there was no hint of movement anywhere on the grass.

He kept asking himself whether they would wait to attack just before dawn. Or would they come any time? Maybe they wouldn't come at all. Maybe it was all bluff, the wishful thinking of men who didn't have the guts to do what they really wanted to do.

No, that was wrong. A year ago it might have been bluff, but not now. Charlie Gilbert made the difference. They'd come, all right. Tomorrow night if not tonight. He groaned, appalled by the prospect of waiting. If it had to come, he wanted it to come now and to be finished with it.

He decided to keep checking with Shaniko when he went to the corral. He'd ask: "Anything doing?"

"Not a damned thing," Shaniko would answer.

Then another circle, the same question, the same answer. Once, as he passed the porch, Vida's voice came to him: "You sure they'll come?"

"Yes, I'm sure."

"Why are you so sure?"

He thought about that a moment. The first answer that came to him was a simple one. He'd been warned by Nider, then by Grant, and finally by Dr. Ripple. But it wouldn't have been the full truth. His feeling of certainty stemmed from something deeper. He searched his mind, and, when he could not put his finger on anything more definite than a feeling that was in him, he said: "Just a hunch, I reckon."

But she wasn't satisfied. "It must be more than that."

"No, it's a hunch. Dad's overdue to collect on his cussedness."

"Only we're the ones who'll collect," Vida said.

"That's right," he agreed, pleased to discover that she was thinking exactly as he was, this twin sister who had been so far from him for so long.

"He says you're crazy to stay up and lose your sleep," Vida went on. "He claims they're too yellow to make a move, but he's just talking, Bill. He got up a while ago, when I was out of the room, and got his rifle and took it to bed with him."

"I thought he couldn't get up."

"Well, he can," she said. "That's what worries Doc. Dad will have to be a lot worse off than he is to stay in bed."

Bill went on around the house again, leaving her standing there. He found a perverse satisfaction in what she had said. Old Mike knew what was going to happen, all right. He wouldn't admit anything, but he knew. Perhaps that was why he had wanted to die before this. He didn't want to be here to harvest the crop he had sowed. If that was true, Old Mike Varney wasn't as tough and brave a man as he made out.

Shaniko heard them coming. He ran from the barn, shouting, "John! Birnie! Soon Hee! Wake up. Get to hell out of that bunkhouse."

Bill sprinted around the house to the front. He heard them,

then, the roar of the pounding hoofs of a dozen horses, coming in from the rim. As he wheeled toward the house, a flash of lightning showed Dutch John, Birnie Hanks, and the cook racing toward the house. If Shaniko had been right in his analysis of how they would make the attack, Charlie Gilbert was leading them, not Phil Nider.

Bill was the last to reach the house. He slammed and barred the door, calling: "Shaniko! John! Take the back! Birnie, stay here with me! Vida, hug the floor!"

Soon Hee had disappeared. Hiding in the pantry or some closet, Bill thought. He heard Old Mike bellow from the bedroom: "What the hell's going on?" He didn't answer. He stood beside a window, looking out. Suddenly, in a quick flash of insight, he knew how Charlie Gilbert felt when his buildings were burned. If Gilbert had his way, there wouldn't be a Pitchfork building left by morning.

They split somewhere in front of the house, one column going right, one left, and, with the house partly circled, they opened up, making the night hideous with rifle fire. Bullets slapped into the stout log walls, some slicing through the windows to bury themselves into the opposite wall of the room. Powder flame winked in quick, orange flashes and was gone, and came again.

Bill fired. So did Birnie. Vida grabbed a rifle off the table in the center of the room and ran to another window. A moment later Shaniko and Dutch John cut loose from the back. Nothing to shoot at except the flash of rifle fire. Lightning made the yard as bright as day and was gone, but in that instant Bill was sure he glimpsed Turk Allen among their assailants.

An instant later Allen's voice sailed out of the darkness: "Varney, I've got something to say! Can you hear me?"

"Go ahead," Bill said.

"We'll give you three minutes to get Vida out of the house.

We ain't fighting women and we don't want her hurt."

From behind Bill, Vida said: "Tell him to go to hell."

"She says to go to hell!" Bill shouted.

He didn't know Old Mike was out of bed until the front door opened and he heard his father's voice. "You're a bunch of yellow bastards. You're with the wrong bunch, Turk. Come in here and fight on your own side."

Bill yelled: "Shut the door!"

And Vida: "Get back into bed, Dad."

Suicide! Sheer, stupid suicide! And yet Bill was never sure that Old Mike really sought death. No one had ever stood up to him. Usually it had been enough to see him, or hear him. Perhaps, in his arrogance, he thought that all he had to do was to stand there and let them hear his voice and they'd go scurrying off the mesa like rabbits running for their holes. To him it was inconceivable that Pitchfork would actually be attacked.

If that was what he thought, he could not have been more wrong. Charlie Gilbert bellowed an oath. He shouted: "Come on, let's go get him!"

Shaniko ran into the front room from the back of the house. Vida rushed toward the open doorway where Old Mike stood, but Bill grabbed her and pushed her against the wall. "Get down," he said. "I told you to hug the floor."

They drove straight for the front of the house, throwing a storm of bullets at Old Mike. A terrific streak of lightning burned the sky, striking somewhere not far away. The thunder that came a second later shook the house, momentarily drowning the sound of gunfire.

Shaniko and Birnie were at two of the windows, firing as fast as they could pull triggers and lever shells into the chambers again. Old Mike must have been hit at once. He was down by the time Bill got to him. He pulled him back into the room and slammed the door and barred it. He ran back to the window and emptied his rifle.

The charge carried the attacking party almost to the porch, horses massed so closely that the gunfire from the house was bound to be effective even in the darkness. There was a moment of confusion, yells and curses and screams of agony and plunging horses. Then they broke and fled. When the next flash of lightning came, Bill saw that three men lay motionlessly in front of the house.

The silence that followed was a strange contrast to the medley of sound that had been there only a moment before. No firing now. Just the receding pound of hoofs and the acrid smell of burned gunpowder.

Vida, kneeling beside Old Mike, was crying. She said: "He's dead, Bill. He's dead."

He kneeled beside her, cupping a match flame above Old Mike's face. He was dead, all right, with at least three bullets in him. Bill blew out the match, and, picking up his father's limp body, carried it into the bedroom and put it down on the bed.

Vida followed him and stood there, still crying, and it came to Bill as he stepped back and put an arm around her that it was a strange and horrible thing that he felt no sorrow, no regret at his father's death.

Old Mike died as he had lived, domineering, egotistical, never doubting his power over others, never doubting that he would be obeyed as he had been obeyed for so many years. But he had been entirely lacking in one thing—the capacity to love.

Now, to Bill's intense regret, he found that he, too, lacked the capacity to love his father. There would be no one, then, to grieve for him except Vida. A sorry way to die, Bill thought, and yet it was the inevitable end of a sorry life.

"He was trying to save us, wasn't he?" Vida asked.

Old Mike never had any such idea in his mind, but Bill knew Vida would feel better if he lied, so he said—"Sure, he tried."—

and went back into the other room.

"Reckon they had enough?" Birnie asked.

"Not with Turk Allen and Charlie Gilbert out there," Bill said.

"I'm going to see who we got," Shaniko said.

Bill reloaded his rifle and stood at a window while Shaniko lifted the bar and slipped out through the front door. Bill hadn't expected this kind of attack. Again he remembered what Shaniko had said would happen if Phil Nider led them, so apparently Nider had stayed behind in Broken Nose where he would be safe.

Nider was a sly, careful man, never taking any risk he could avoid, but Charlie Gilbert was entirely different. He would have burned the buildings if he'd had time, but Old Mike's voice must have fanned his hatred into a crazy passion that hungered for his enemy's death. So Gilbert, giving way to that passion, had spontaneously changed his plan. Now three of them were dead. There would be no more charges like that. The next move would be to fire the buildings.

Bill remained at the window, expecting to see a tongue of flame streak up into the darkness from the barn or some of the sheds. But he could see nothing except during the occasional flickers of lightning. Presently Shaniko returned, and shut and barred the front door.

"Three of 'em," he said. "Deader'n hell. The closest one to the porch is Charlie Gilbert." Shaniko picked up his rifle and reloaded. Then he added: "It's starting to rain."

"Maybe they'll pull out," Birnie said, "with Charlie gone."

"No," Shaniko said. "Not if Turk can hold 'em. He ain't gonna be satisfied until he gets his hands on Vida."

Shaniko went back to where he had been stationed in the rear of the house. The firing began again, but this time from a distance. No movement out there. They must have dismounted.

Bullets ripped into the outside walls. A few snapped through the windows, knocking out bits of glass that remained. No sense in answering the fire, Bill decided. Probably each man had found some sort of protection, or was lying flat on his belly.

Suddenly the rain came in a downpour, running off the roof in a stream. A minute out there in a storm like this would soak a man to his hide. For a moment Bill had a wild and futile hope that the rain would dampen their spirits enough to make them pull out.

Charlie Gilbert had been the driving force behind the attack. Phil Nider had had his part in it, too, but it had been Gilbert, Bill was sure, who had ramrodded the fight. It had been his fury and his compulsive desire for revenge that had built the fire in the hearts of the south mesa ranchers. Now Charlie Gilbert was dead.

Still the desultory fire continued. They wouldn't leave, Bill decided, even with Gilbert gone. It might take Ed Grant and the rest of the Pitchfork hands from the Flat Tops to lift the siege. The south mesa men would lie out there on their bellies like drowned rats, but they'd stay.

Now, Bill thought, Turk Allen would be giving the orders. It would be Turk Allen who would hold them together. His plans had failed, he had taken a beating, and he resembled Charlie Gilbert in the sense that he was not a man to forget an injury.

So the night wore on toward the morning, the rain hammering down, a rifle cracking now and then just to show the defenders that their enemies had not withdrawn. Presently Bill asked Vida to make some coffee. A moment later she ran back into the front room. "Bill, Shaniko's gone."

He wheeled from the window where he had been standing. "Gone? Where?"

"I don't know. He's just gone."

Bill crossed the room, calling: "John?"

Dutch John said: "I ain't going nowhere."

"Where's Shaniko?"

"Dunno. He left a long time ago. Told me to bar the back door behind him."

"What the hell did you let him go for?"

"You ever try to stop Shaniko when he got his head set on anything?" Dutch John asked mildly.

"Yeah, I've tried," Bill said. "That was a fool question. Did he say what he figured on doing?"

"No."

Bill returned to the other room. That was a foolish question, too. Shaniko wouldn't say why he was going, but Bill knew. Shaniko wouldn't be back until Turk Allen was dead. The chances were good that he wouldn't be back at all. There was nothing to do but stand here at the window and curse himself for not using a gun on Turk Allen instead of his fists.

Vida brought coffee to Bill and Birnie. The rain still rattled on the roof, but there had been no firing for a long time. Vida asked fretfully: "Whatever possessed Shaniko to do a crazy thing like that?"

"If you really knew Shaniko, you'd understand," Bill said. "Neither you nor me would be safe with Turk alive. Shaniko aims to fix that."

Vida whirled away and went into the kitchen. Bill stared out into the darkness, and presently a faint morning glow came to the rain-drenched mesa. Shaniko Red was a one-woman man. Maybe Vida would never have him. He didn't really expect it, Bill thought, but he'd go on loving her just the same and he'd never marry anyone else.

Dutch John called: "Bill, he's coming in! Ain't enough light to be sure, but I think it's him."

Bill joined Dutch John at a kitchen window. He heard Shaniko call: "Don't shoot! It's me!"

Bill lifted the bar and, opening the door, called: "Come in. What the hell you been up to?"

"You come out here," Shaniko said. "Shut the door."

Bill stepped outside, closing the door behind him. A moment later Shaniko appeared. He said in a matter-of-fact voice: "Turk's dead. I bellied around in the mud till I found him. I had to knife him or I'd had the whole bunch on top of me. The rest of 'em rode off."

That was like Shaniko. No heroics. No brag. Now he was back and he didn't expect any thanks or compliments. Bill laid a hand on his shoulder. "You did a good job."

"There wasn't much sand in their craw," Shaniko said. "Not with Charlie Gilbert and Turk Allen out of it. I wasn't very far from Turk when they found him. Scared 'em stiff. They said a damned Injun was amongst 'em and they'd all get knifed if they stayed, so they lit a shuck for town."

"Town? You heard them say that?"

"Yeah, Sid Kehoe did. They was scared Ed Grant would throw 'em into the calaboose, so they was gonna see Phil Nider."

"You stay here. With Vida." Bill opened the door into the kitchen, calling: "Birnie!" When Birnie Hanks appeared from the front of the house, Bill said: "You 'n' me are going to town. John, I want you to stay with Shaniko and Vida."

"What are you going to do?" Vida demanded. "Haven't we gone through enough?"

"No," Bill said. "Not yet. This has got to be finished now, and then there'll be no more trouble on this range."

He went out into the pale dawn light and crossed the muddy yard to the corral, with Birnie beside him. The rain had stopped, and already the clouds were breaking away. They saddled up and took the road to town.

Vida had lit a lamp in the house. As Bill rode past, he told himself he'd have to fetch some windows from town to replace the ones that had been shot out. Then he thought: *If I'm still alive to fetch anything back from town.*

CHAPTER TWENTY-ONE

Bill was uncertain about what would happen when he reached town. His main object was to convince the men who were left that there would be no more trouble, that if the south mesa ranchers would stay on their side of the river, Pitchfork would stay on its side. With Old Mike dead, Bill could guarantee peace—if Sid Kehoe and Pete Matts and the rest wanted peace.

The one man who fastened himself in Bill's thoughts like a cockle burr in a horse's tail was Phil Nider. What would he do, now that Charlie Gilbert and Turk Allen were dead?

Nider had succeeded in staying out of the fight, but Dr. Ripple had said he'd finally taken a stand against Pitchfork. Would he retreat from that stand, or would he, by the same devious means he had been using, try to keep the fight going? Or would he try something himself?

Nider could have been the man who had shot Old Mike from the ridge. He had small feet, he wasn't a cigarette smoker, and he certainly had the patience to wait up there on the ridge until Old Mike appeared. He could have been the one who had tried to knife Bill in the hotel room. He filled the bill as far as size was concerned.

Bill kept revolving it around in his mind as he rode down the mesa hill to the river. The sun was beginning to show. The clouds had broken away, the storm was moving on east, and for a time the horizon flamed with the sunrise. Bill and Birnie reached the bottom and took the road to Broken Nose, pulling their hat brims down against the harsh, slanted rays of the sun.

Bill felt reasonably sure he could handle men like Sid Kehoe and Pete Matts, if Nider stayed out of it. But probably he wouldn't. He had hated Old Mike. Perhaps he hated Bill because of Marian Tracey. Still, he didn't seem to fit the pattern that Bill's thoughts kept fashioning for him. He was a store-keeper who had a talent for making money, a precise, methodical man who apparently was interested only in running his business and dressing neatly and being looked after in his fine house by a housekeeper. How serious was he, then, in wanting to marry Marian? Bill had no way of knowing.

One of two things must be true. Either Bill was completely wrong in his thinking, mentally accusing Nider of vicious acts that he had not done, or he was a different man from the serene and quiet merchant he appeared to be. Bill could not decide which was true. He was still thinking about it when he met Dr. Ripple just west of town.

The doctor pulled up his buggy and motioned for Bill and Birnie to stop. He was tired and disheveled and nervous. Even his voice showed the pressure he was under when he said: "I was going after you. You sure raised hell last night."

"We showed 'em," Birnie said jubilantly. "They got more'n they looked for."

"Four men dead," Ripple said. "Two of the others have got head wounds. One of them with a broken arm. Another with a bullet gash along his ribs."

"We had to defend ourselves," Bill said, thinking he was be-ing censured. "They'd have wiped us out if we'd let them."

"I'm not blaming you," Ripple said quickly. "The hell of it is the guilty man hasn't been touched and maybe he won't."

"Old Mike's dead," Bill said, and told the doctor how it had happened.

"Old Mike was some to blame, sure," Ripple said, "but I've

173

known him for a long time. I'm not sure he didn't have a reason for doing. . . ." He stopped and shook his head. "That's all water over the dam and there's no sense going back over it. What I'm trying to say is that he was selfish and greedy and plumb blind some ways, but he wouldn't have murdered a woman."

"Woman?" Bill demanded. "What woman?"

"Missus Tracey," Ripple said impatiently as if he thought Bill knew. "Marian's mother." He stopped and pounded the seat beside him. "Trouble is I don't have any proof to give Ed Grant. Not real proof, but I know damned well Phil Nider did it."

"I hadn't heard. . . ."

"Hell, no. I keep forgetting. It happened last night. When Marian was at choir practice. Missus Tracey was alone in the house. That was all right. I'm sure not blaming Marian. Her mother was strong as a horse in spite of all the blubbering she did about how she felt. Choir practice and church on Sunday morning were the only times Marian ever left her. I'd just got back from your place and I went to see her. She was dead. In bed. No marks on her. Apparently she'd died in her sleep. Whoever did it, and I say it was Nider, wanted everybody to think her heart had quit."

"Maybe it did. She's been. . . ."

"No." Ripple shook his head. "Somebody had been there. I think she was smothered to death. Maybe with her pillow. Nider's the one who had the most to gain because he sure didn't want the old lady on his hands when he married Marian. He asked me about her the other night. When I told him she'd live a long time yet, his face fell three feet. That's not like Phil Nider. It's mighty seldom he ever lets you see what he's thinking or how he feels."

Bill looked down at the doctor, the horror of this making him sick. Shooting Old Mike from ambush was bad enough. Coming at Bill with a knife in the middle of the night was just as bad. But smothering an old woman with a pillow was far worse. Again the thought was in Bill's mind that Nider was being falsely accused or he was not the man he had appeared to be.

"It doesn't sound like Nider," Bill said finally.

"Doesn't sound like anybody else, either," the doctor snapped. "I never knew another man like him. You go into his store or you talk to him on the street, and he's real pleasant and polite, but, by God, Bill, you never know what he's thinking. He's a cold son-of-a-bitch."

"I still don't know why you figure she was murdered."

"Her heart wasn't bad. She just didn't have anything wrong with her that would have killed her. Somebody was in her room. A cup of water on the stand was knocked over. Her glasses were on the floor. Marian always left her slippers right under the edge of the bed. When I got there, they were clean over against the wall. Whoever did it must have kicked them. Marian wouldn't have left them where I found them." He spread his hands. "It adds up."

"Well, what do you want me to do?"

"Marian needs you. She's taking it pretty hard. Blames herself for leaving the old lady alone."

"You tell her you think it was Nider?"

"No, but I'm pretty sure she's figured it out. She loves you. Always has. And you love her. Don't try to tell me anything different."

"Sure I love her," Bill said bitterly, "but she promised Nider she'd marry him."

"And why?" Ripple demanded. "I'll tell you, if you haven't got sense enough to figure it out. She couldn't go on the way she was, and she wouldn't burden you with her ma. I'm not sure she would have married Nider when the time came. It was too much, even if she had promised."

"Doc, you want me to go see Marian. Is that what you've been trying to say all this time?"

"Not yet," Ripple said impatiently. "Later. First thing you've got to do is to go after Phil Nider and make him admit he murdered the old lady. With what little I know, Ed Grant can't touch him. You can." Ripple pounded the seat of the buggy again. "Nider's scared of you. You've got as tough as a boot heel lately. Look at your record. Sure, you were forced into it, but the record stands. You brace Nider and he'll crack."

"All right," Bill said, "I'll try."

He rode on with Birnie beside him and Ripple turned his buggy and followed.

The south mesa ranchers were on the street in front of the Stockade. Two had bloody bandages around their heads, and another had his arm in a sling. They saw Bill coming long before he reached the business block, and stood waiting, hands on gun butts. Phil Nider was not among them.

"This is worse'n crazy," Birnie said. "We're walking into a dose of lead poisoning. There's seven of 'em just waiting for us."

Bill dismounted at the end of the block and tied his horse. He said: "I'll go on alone."

"You ain't going alone," Birnie, said, and stepped out of his saddle and tied beside Bill's horse.

Seven of them, Bill thought as he walked slowly toward the Stockade. He searched their faces. They were tired and scared and jumpy. Still, he didn't think there would be any trouble after what had happened at Pitchfork. When he had covered half the distance, he saw that Sid Kehoe was missing.

Pete Matts called: "Stop where you are, Varney! We've had a bellyful, but we ain't gonna stand here and let you knock us over."

Bill halted, motioning for Birnie to stop, too. Seven against two, but the seven were scared. He said: "We didn't come to knock you over. Old Mike's dead. We've had a bellyful, too. No reason for us to fight now. We'll stay north of the river if you'll stay on your side. I came here to tell you that. If we're ever going to have peace, we'll have it now."

They were shocked by the news that Old Mike was dead. To them, as with everyone else on Skull River, Old Mike Varney had seemed as permanent as the cliffs that frowned down upon the valley. They shuffled around, backing up toward the batwings of the Stockade.

Finally Pete Matts said: "You're Old Mike's kid and you've got a sister. I reckon both of you own Pitchfork now, but how do we know you'll keep your word?"

"Whatever we Varneys have done, we haven't lied," Bill said. "You'd better believe me. Ed Grant's on his way here with the rest of our crew. If we have to, we'll sweep the south mesa clean, but we don't want to."

They shuffled again, nervous, jittery, expectant, gradually edging toward the saloon. Then Chauncey Morts crashed through the batwings, yelling: "They saw you coming, Bill! Watch out."

They grabbed him and shoved him back through the door. Only one man remained in front of the bat wings. Sid Kehoe. He hadn't been there a moment before. Bill didn't know where he had come from unless he had been keeping Chauncey Morts inside and had come out behind the saloonman. Bill wouldn't have seen him if he had, for his eyes had been on Morts.

"Yeah, it's a trap, Varney," Kehoe said. "I'm going to kill you. For my brother. Think I'd forget that?"

Something was wrong. This wasn't like Sid Kehoe. One of the others might have the guts to brace Bill, Pete Matts maybe, but not Kehoe.

"I don't want to kill you, Sid," Bill said. "Don't make me."

Kehoe's laugh was a jeering sound. "You're yellow, Varney. We know we've got to get you before Ed Grant shows up. That's why we're still in town. We figured you'd be along. How about your man Hanks? Is he gonna stay out of it?"

"He'll stay out of it," Bill said wearily. "Make your play, Sid."

For just a moment Kehoe hesitated, looking as if he regretted this brashness and was about to break and run. Bill wondered if it would ever end, if the time would come when he would not have to look at an enemy through the smoke of his gun.

Kehoe went for his Colt and Bill made his draw. He had Kehoe beaten. He was sure of it, then a bullet hit him and knocked him into the mud of the street. The sound of the gunshot came before Kehoe's gun flamed

Another shot. Birnie was buying into the fight. Kehoe remained on his feet, firing at Bill, wild bullets that were missing by wide margins. Bill still had his gun in his hand. His left side was paralyzed as if he'd been struck by a club, but he was able to shoot. He knocked Kehoe half around with his first shot and put him down with his second, and still there was more shooting.

He tried to get up and spilled back again into the mud, then he heard Birnie yell: "I got him, Bill! I got that back-shooting bastard! He was up there on the store roof."

Dr. Ripple was running along the walk, yelling: "Nider! He had it all worked out with Kehoe! Timing their shots so it would look like Kehoe did it!"

That was all Bill remembered until he came to in Dr. Ripple's office. A lot of men were there—Birnie Hanks and Ed Grant and the Pitchfork boys from the Flat Tops. Grant was saying: "I'll arrest the whole bunch. They'll go to the pen for the rest of their lives for making that raid."

"No," Bill said. "Let them go. There won't be any more trouble."

178

"Why, hell, man, they. . . ."

"Let them go," Bill said. "You boys had your ride for nothing. The trouble's over."

They drifted out, Grant still grumbling, and it was not until the room was cleared that he saw Marian. She came to him, pulled up a chair, and, sitting down beside the cot, took one of his hands. She had been crying and he remembered her mother. He wanted to say something to comfort her, to tell her he was sorry, but he couldn't put his tongue to the words.

Instead, he said: "I love you."

That was all, just the three words, but they were the right words. She squeezed his hand and tried to smile, unable to say anything. At this moment, there was no need for her to speak. She loved him. He saw it in her eyes, in the sweet set of her mouth, and that was all the assurance he needed.

The season of death was passed.

ABOUT THE AUTHOR

Wayne D. Overholser won three Spur Awards from the Western Writers of America and has a long list of fine Western titles to his credit. He was born in Pomeroy, Washington, and attended the University of Montana, University of Oregon, and the University of Southern California before becoming a public schoolteacher and principal in various Oregon communities. He began writing for Western pulp magazines in 1936 and within a couple of years was a regular contributor to Street & Smith's *Western Story Magazine* and Fiction House's *Lariat Story Magazine*. *Buckaroo's Code* (1947) was his first Western novel and remains one of his best. In the 1950s and 1960s, having retired from academic work to concentrate on writing, he would publish as many as four books a year under his own name or a pseudonym, most prominently as Joseph Wayne. *The Violent Land* (1954), *The Lone Deputy* (1957), *The Bitter Night* (1961), and *Riders of the Sundowns* (1997) are among the finest of the Overholser titles. *The Sweet and Bitter Land* (1950), *Bunch Grass* (1955), and *Land of Promises* (1962) are among the best Joseph Wayne titles, and *Law Man* (1953) is a most rewarding novel under the Lee Leighton pseudonym. Overholser's Western novels, whatever the byline, are based on a solid knowledge of the history and customs of the 19th-Century West, particularly when set in his two favorite Western states, Oregon and Colorado. Many of his novels are first-person narratives, a technique that tends to bring an added dimension of vividness to the frontier experiences of his narrators and frequently, as in *Cast a Long Shadow* (1957), the female characters one encounters are among the most memorable. He wrote his numerous novels with a consistent skill and an uncommon sensitivity to the depths of human character. Almost invariably, his stories weave a spell of their own with their scenes and images of social and economic forces often in conflict and the diverse ways of life and personalities that made the American Western frontier so unique a time and place in human history.